CREAT NORTHERN RAILWAY

JAMES J. HILL

CULVER PICTURES

MEYER GUGGENHEIM

BROWN BROTHERS

JAMES B. DUKE

CAPTAINS

JOHN D. ROCKEFELLER

BROWN BROTHERS

J. P. MORGAN

STATE HISTORICAL SOCIETY OF WISCONSIN

CYRUS H. McCORMICK

PHILIP D. ARMOUR

ANDREW CARNEGIE   HENRY FORD   CORNELIUS VANDERBILT

OF INDUSTRY

BY THE EDITORS OF
AMERICAN HERITAGE
The Magazine of History

AUTHOR
BERNARD A. WEISBERGER

CONSULTANT
ALLAN NEVINS
Professor Emeritus of American History, Columbia University

PUBLISHED BY
AMERICAN HERITAGE PUBLISHING CO., INC.

BOOK TRADE AND INSTITUTIONAL DISTRIBUTION BY
HARPER & ROW

FIRST EDITION

© 1966 by American Heritage Publishing Co., Inc., 551 Fifth
Avenue, New York, New York 10017. All rights reserved under
Bern and Pan-American Copyright Conventions. Library of Con-
gress Catalog Card Number: 66-17232. Trademark AMERICAN
HERITAGE JUNIOR LIBRARY registered United States Patent Office.

Wall Street, where Stock Exchange bids could win or lose fortunes in a few hours, often witnessed panics such as this, in 1857, when overinflated stocks collapsed.

FOREWORD

The United States entered the nineteenth century as a quiet land of family farms, villages, and a few small cities clustered along the Atlantic seaboard. By the end of the century it was well on the way to becoming the mightiest industrial power in the world, with teeming cities, humming factories, and great agricultural complexes in a nation stretching from sea to sea. *Captains of Industry* is the story of the men who made possible this enormous transformation.

It took intelligence, imagination, and determination to make a mark on those brawling times, but if a man was shrewd and persistent enough—and if he had more than a little luck—his reward could be money in quantities undreamed of by previous generations.

In the decades after the Civil War, the names to contend with in American life were those of Guggenheim, Hill, Armour, Duke, Rockefeller, and other masters of finance and industry. More influential than the nation's elected leaders, they formed an aristocracy of wealth in a land that had taken pride in the equal rights of all its citizens. Business, as historian Allan Nevins has observed, became the field "to which the majority of Americans looked for distinction, authority, and self expression. A whole generation pushed into it partly for money, partly for the satisfaction of successful competitive effort, partly for eminence and power."

The ten captains of industry in this book shared, even as young men, an ability to size up a situation and shape their actions accordingly. Vanderbilt's farsighted decision that steam was the coming thing was reached when he was twenty-two; McCormick was twenty-one when he designed the reaper that brought him fame; and Carnegie was seventeen when he sent out orders to untangle a railroad wreck in his employer's absence. Ford was not yet twenty when he abandoned the idea of becoming a watchmaker "because I figured out that watches were not universal necessities, and therefore people generally would not buy them. . . . I wanted to make something in quantity."

Few of them ever lost the capacity for instant decision. Sixty-three-year-old J. P. Morgan, when solicited for a donation to Harvard University's new medical school, glanced for a moment at the plans unrolled on his office table. Then he stabbed down three times with his finger: "I will build that, and that, and that. Good morning, gentlemen." One minute to spend a million dollars.

Like other aristocrats, the captains of industry often abused their privileges. Their blunt and forceful methods of doing business raised storms of protest from those who were exploited in the process. Historians and journalists—and eventually legislators—of the late nineteenth century indicted many of America's industrial titans as "robber barons." Following generations, while still condemning the most ruthless of these men, have reached a new appreciation of their role in building industrial America and thereby bringing security, hope, and prosperity to its people.

The Editors

RIGHT: *A mid-nineteenth century bank note proudly depicts the age's new marvels: the railroad, the reaper, the power loom, and the steamship.*

PRINTS DIVISION, N. Y. PUBLIC LIBRARY

COVER: *Workers in an iron foundry inspired J. F. Weir to interpret the strength and vigor of the Industrial Revolution in a dramatic painting.*

PUTNAM COUNTY HISTORICAL SOCIETY: COURTESY *Life* © TIME INC.

FRONT ENDSHEET: *The Homestead Steel Mill in 1884 nestled in a Pennsylvania valley into which Pittsburgh's chimneys were already encroaching.*

CHARLES J. ROSENBLOOM

BACK ENDSHEET: *This 1911 cartoon from* Life, *a humor magazine, contrived to satirize almost every character then renowned on Wall Street.*

Life, OCTOBER 26, 1911

BACK COVER: *Smoking New Hampshire cotton mills and a gaudy woodburning locomotive symbolize the growing use of steam power in 1856.*

OLD PRINT SHOP

CONTENTS

1
THE COMMODORE AND THE IRON HORSE

By 1878 distant sections of the country were linked by the power of steam. In this painting of a Prov

In the summer of 1810, a sixteen-year-old boy who lived on Staten Island in New York harbor decided to go into the shipping business. He persuaded his mother to lend him $100 out of the precious family savings and bought a "periauger"—a tiny boat with two masts and a flat bottom. Then the lad offered a ferry service between Staten Island and the lower tip of Manhattan, five miles away. The fare was eighteen cents each way, and a quarter for the round trip. Every day the little boat left on schedule, and despite tricky tides, choppy waves, and high winds, it was rarely late. The work was wet and hard. It was also the cornerstone of a career for young Cornelius Vanderbilt.

In those days, barely one hundred

ence wharf, cotton is loaded from a southern steamer onto boxcars bound for New England mills.

thousand people lived in New York. James Madison was President of the United States, the fourth man to hold the office that he himself had helped to write into the Constitution. Cities like Buffalo, Cincinnati, and St. Louis were rough frontier settlements; Chicago did not even exist. The West of forest and Indian began at the Alleghenies, at some points less than one hundred miles inland from the Atlantic coast. Most Americans lived on farms, wore homespun clothing, read by oil lamps, and warmed themselves at wood fires. Men and goods moved by the power of wind and animal muscle, at speeds of under ten miles per hour. It took two full days to make the ninety-mile trip from New York to Philadelphia.

By the time Vanderbilt died, nearly seventy years later, the steam engine had changed the face of the land. Steam provided a new and gigantic source of power that men could add to their own as they toiled to unlock the hidden treasure of the American continent. Steam engines could power a threshing machine in an Iowa harvest field, a drill excavating a copper mine in Montana, or a loom spinning cotton yarn into cloth in a Rhode Island textile factory. Steam locomotives, hurtling over a network of railroads, could bring the products of one area to fill the needs of another. Farm produce from the prairies, bales of cotton and tobacco from the South, factory-made goods from the East, mineral ores from Minnesota and the Rockies, crisscrossed the country. Most important of all, the trains carried people. First came pioneers, prospectors, and men looking for quick money. Then came immigrants, families with children, looking for a place to settle down, and get to work on turning their dreams into reality. But faster than the crack trains, which now could carry passengers the nine hundred miles from New York to Chicago in a little over twenty-four hours, traveled the electric spark of the telegraph, which could rap out a message in San Francisco and New York simultaneously. That message was the herald of a new and equally marvelous age—that of electricity.

In 1877, the year of Vanderbilt's death, the telegraph was already thirty years old, the telephone had just been invented, and practical electric motors and electric lights were just around the corner. In another twenty years gasoline engines would be applied to transportation. Then men would travel at ever-increasing speeds over an ever-improving network of roads, with no need to be bothered with boilers and rails. But why bother with keeping to the roads? And so, eventually, men took to the air, powering their airplanes with highly developed gasoline engines. The era of steam was only the opening chapter in the story of a modern world.

Millions of men helped bring this new world to birth: inventors and scientists, soldiers and statesmen, pioneer settlers and industrial laborers.

This steam plant and paddle wheel assembly, sketched by inventor Robert Fulton, powered his Clermont, *which in 1807 became America's first dependable steamship and herald of a new age.*

There were also a small number of men who made it their task to organize the work of others. They brought the savings of a rapidly growing population—or investment capital, in the language of economics—into working patterns with the new machines and the old raw materials. In doing so, many of them created giant industrial and transportation empires. Because it all happened so quickly and on such a vast scale, these so-called captains of industry grew rich and powerful almost overnight. They were, like characters in a fairy tale, gifted with the magic powers of imagination and ability, with necessity playing the part of fairy godmother. Like all men who gain control over others, they were both respected and feared: admired by those who envied their dynamic drive, or hated by those who were ruined by their determination to make money and to get ahead, whatever the cost. Few of these larger-than-life-size men found time in their busy lives for reflection or gentleness. Some of them, in their impatient strength, threatened the values of equal opportunity and government by law and consent which support American democracy at its best. Yet all of them, good and bad alike, made important contributions to national growth.

13

Vanderbilt's first command was a periauger like the one at right. Within 25 years he was commodore of a fleet of steamships on Long Island Sound. Pride of his fleet was the 488-ton Lexington, *above, called "the fastest boat that ever sailed, speed 23 miles an hour when drove up." In 1840 the five-year-old ship burned with a loss of 200 lives.*

14

Steam was far from the mind of Cornelius Vanderbilt (or Van Derbilt, as he usually spelled his name) at the start. Young "Cornele the boatman" was busy building a reputation as the ablest and hardest working ferry operator in New York harbor. Between ferry trips he found freight-hauling assignments, and he was prepared to tackle any job in any weather. Once, during a storm which kept his competitors hugging the wharves, he was asked if he could bring some officers into the city from the fort at Sandy Hook, at the entrance to the lower bay of New York. "Yes," he replied cheerfully, "but I shall have to carry them under water part of the way." He was as good as his word: his passengers arrived safely, but soaked to the skin.

The War of 1812 brought a brisk demand for vessels to carry troops and stores to the various forts defending New York's harbor. Cornelius worked around the clock, paying his parents all the money he earned in the daytime and half his earnings at night. He thriftily set aside the other half in savings, and by the time peace came he had enough money to buy a little coasting schooner. Gradually, he acquired complete or part ownership of six little ships which heeled along the coast bringing oysters, fish, and vegetables to market. By 1817 "Cornele" had married his cousin, had put aside $9,000 in cash, and seemed to have a fine career ahead as a merchant loading square-riggers for distant seas.

Vanderbilt was one of the first of these colossal, colorful figures. By wise investment, shrewd manipulation, and the use of his fists when need be, he built up a fortune of almost $100,000,000, and died the richest man in the United States. His life was, as one biographer put it, an "epic of the steam age."

But his mind was working differently. Cornelius liked sailboats, but sensed that the "b'ilers," as he called them, that had recently begun to puff around New York harbor had a future full of promise. He planned to take part in developing that future.

The way was not a simple one. Early steamboats were clumsy, cranky inventions. They broke down or blew up frequently, and they were expensive. So Vanderbilt decided to educate himself in the ways of steam on water without investing his own money at the start. Instead, he hired himself out to a wealthy New Jerseyite, Thomas Gibbons, as captain of a steamboat that Gibbons operated between New York and New Brunswick, New Jersey. (From there, travelers went by coach to Trenton, and then by water again down the Delaware to Philadelphia.) Vanderbilt's first steamship was meekly called the *Mouse*, but his job on it was exciting. Gibbons was competing with a rival line, which had secured, from New York State, the exclusive right to carry people between New York and New Jersey. Thus, in the eyes of his native state, Cornelius was breaking the law each time he landed in Manhattan, and he found that he had to be nimble to avoid being arrested. Sometimes he was not nimble enough. As he once reported to Gibbons in his rough-and-ready spelling: "This day J.R. [one of the owners of the rival line that was chartered by New York State] brought a sute agaits all my men even the

kook but caught no boddy but me."

Nevertheless, he kept on with his business of mastering steamboats and graduated to the command of a bigger ship, the *Bellona*, on the same run. Gibbons meanwhile embarked on a series of lawsuits against his rival. Finally, in 1824, in the case of *Gibbons v. Ogden*, the United States Supreme Court ruled that the legislature of New York had been in the wrong. No state could grant a monopoly—in other words, give one man or firm complete control—of traffic between any two states. Power over interstate commerce belonged only to Congress. The way was thus open for many independent steamship operators, without political influence, to develop interstate runs. Five years after the decision, Vanderbilt — now thirty-five, with savings of over $30,000 — resigned from Gibbons' employ and became his own master again. His battles on Gibbons' behalf had taught him a few things by hard experience. Money, lawsuits, and the right connections with lawmakers were useful aids to business success. Monopolies could be dangerous enemies—unless you happened to own them yourself.

For the next twenty years Vanderbilt operated steamers in New York Bay, on the Hudson River, and finally on Long Island Sound. He was a fierce competitor, prepared to cut fares of two or three dollars down to ten cents when fighting for passengers. Competing owners soon learned that in such ruinous price wars it was never

Vanderbilt who backed down first. They paid him, finally, to withdraw from business between New York and New Jersey, and on the Hudson. (Of course when he did so, they promptly raised fares again to cover their losses, so that in the long run the public paid for the competition. But the business practices of the time were less strictly controlled than now, and such behavior was not exceptional.) On Long Is-

When the Commodore posed for Matthew Brady during the Civil War, his ships had brought him over $20,000,000.

land Sound, however, Vanderbilt's ships became a familiar sight. Long, narrow at both ends, with tall smoke stacks thickly belching black wood-smoke, and huge gilt paddle-boxes, they carried passengers in luxury from New York to points in Connecticut and Rhode Island, and eventually all the way to Boston.

Soon, New York papers were referring to Vanderbilt as "the Commodore"—one who commands a large fleet—and the name stuck. He was an important citizen, helping his city to build up a profitable and growing trade with New England and the interior. It was time to move to Manhattan. His wife at first objected to leaving their fine house on Staten Island, but Vanderbilt committed her to a private mental asylum for a couple of months to think things over and she withdrew her opposition. In 1846 the Vanderbilts moved into a fashionable new house off Washington Square, and the Commodore bought fast trotting horses to take him on Sunday drives. He worked hard and enjoyed his money, but he was never quite accepted by the older society of New York. After all, he had once worked as a boatman; he still swore like a dockhand, murdered Webster's English, and refused to be respectable. At the age of fifty, he got into a street brawl which developed during a political parade, and successfully knocked out a prize fighter.

The Commodore was tough, as those who crossed him soon found

18 *New York, as seen in this 1847 view, was America's major port, thanks to its incompa-rable deep-water harbor (upper left) and two easily navigable waterways: the Hudsor*

(background) and the East River (foreground), which provided plenty of dock space. Steaming down the bustling East River is the Commodore's flagship, the C. Vanderbilt.

19

out. In 1850, for example, during the California Gold Rush, he joined with others in forming a company to set up a new route from New York to San Francisco. This meant going by ocean steamer to the east coast of Nicaragua, then across that country by lake and river boat and muleback to the Pacific, then northward again by sea. (Vanderbilt even went to Central America and laid out the Nicaraguan inland water route, scaring his engineers by tying down safety valves to raise enough steam to force his boats through rapids and over sandbars.) After a couple of years of operation, two fellow directors of this company took advantage of Vanderbilt's absence on a trip abroad to buy control of the management through stock purchases. They then tried to break their agreements with the Commodore. When he returned and found out about it, he dictated a letter. It read: "Gentlemen: You have undertaken to cheat me. I won't sue you, for the law is too slow. I'll ruin you."

Promptly, he opened a competing line by way of the Isthmus of Panama, cutting fares for a five-thousand-mile trip to as little as thirty dollars for steerage. Soon, the Nicaraguan route was almost abandoned, and the company that ran it was on the verge of bankruptcy. Vanderbilt bought his way back into the company and took pleasure in seeing his rivals ousted. They later made a deal with the dictator of Nicaragua—an American soldier of fortune named

Early gold seekers traveled by native dugout on a five-day trip across Panama. Vanderbilt introduced steamers to Central America.

William Walker—to seize the Vanderbilt properties in the country. The relentless Commodore then lent his support to an invasion by Honduras, Guatemala, San Salvador, and Costa Rica which threw Walker out. The influence of the modern world, and of American capital, was already strong enough to be felt in jungles thousands of miles from home.

These Central American operations and the establishment of a transatlantic line occupied Vanderbilt throughout the 1850's. By the time the Civil War broke out, however, he was ready to bid steamships goodbye. Nearly seventy, but still hale, Vanderbilt was now prepared to bet everything he had on the new king of the transportation world, the iron horse. At that point, "everything he had" amounted to something between ten and twenty million dollars.

Vanderbilt's first experience with railroads had not been happy. In 1833 he was riding a Camden & Amboy Railroad train to Philadelphia, when an axle broke and his carriage overturned. He was pitched down a thirty-foot embankment and was lucky to survive, despite broken ribs and a punctured lung. Nevertheless, he had confidence in the potential of railroads and started buying railroad stocks some years before 1863, which was the year he became president of the New York & Harlem Railroad. This little line did a small business in commuter traffic and the transport of farm goods in the Bronx and Westchester County. Its real importance to Vanderbilt was that it had good terminal facilities in New York City. His eye was on bigger game, however. The Hudson River Railroad, on the east side of the river for which it was named, joined New York to Albany. There it connected with another line, the New York Central, which carried the rich freight of the West eastward from Buffalo. By biding his time and buying carefully, Vanderbilt finally got enough shares of Hudson River stock to make him the effective owner of the line. He could be sure that, as owner of more than half of the stock,

his orders would be strictly obeyed.

With the Hudson River line in his grasp, Vanderbilt controlled all the rail traffic into New York. Now his problem was to work with—or against—the New York Central. To arrange for their freight to be picked up at Albany, the owners of that line could make a number of different and advantageous arrangements: with Hudson River steamboats, or with Vanderbilt's line, or even with the Western Railroad, which ran from Albany to Boston. But Vanderbilt did not like to dance to the Central's tune. By severe rate-cutting, he managed to reduce riverboat competition, and he made

In 1839 rival transporters warned the public about the railroad on which Vanderbilt took his first—and nearly last—train ride.

temporary pacts with the Central. But these pacts were never binding; they could be canceled whenever the lordly Central wanted to make a better deal. In January of 1867, when the Commodore thought that the Central had backed out of an arrangement with him, he took a drastic step. He ordered the trains of his Hudson River line to be stopped at East Albany, on the opposite bank of the river from the terminal in Albany where the Central's tracks ended. No boats were running in the ice-choked river, of course. Passengers bound for New York from the north and west had to trudge through snowdrifts to change trains, and freight had to be hauled in the same bitter way. Public opinion was enraged—not only with Vanderbilt but also with the Central. Yet the Central could not afford to lose public confidence, for it was fighting severe competition from several other major lines or "trunks" between the Atlantic and the Great Lakes. So, when the price of New York Central dropped sharply on the stock market, a group of Central stockholders decided that the way out lay not in fighting Vanderbilt, but in joining him. They gave the Commodore control over their votes (which represented $13,000,000 worth of stock) and elected him president of the board of directors. Vanderbilt ruled the rails from New York all the way to Buffalo.

The power that Vanderbilt commanded was vividly symbolized by this incident. A railroad king was a

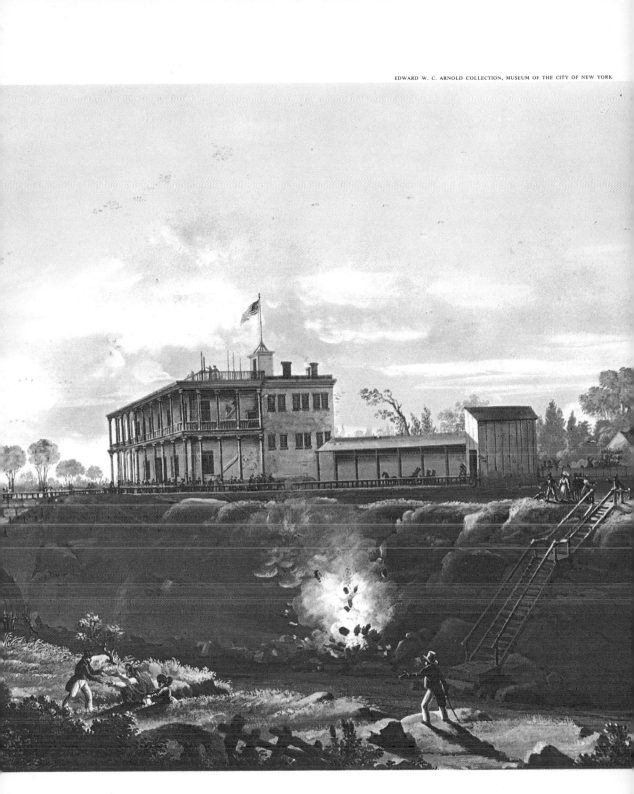

Nicolino Calyo painted New York & Harlem Railroad workers blasting a roadbed through Manhattan in 1836. Forty years later this section was sunk below the level of Park Avenue.

king indeed. Henry Adams, himself a descendant of two Presidents, looked hard at Vanderbilt in 1869 and was disturbed. "His ambition," he wrote, "is a great one. It seems to be nothing less than to make himself master in his own right of the great channels of communication which connect the city of New York with the interior of the continent, and to control them as his private property." The Commodore, Adams went on, had sought "to make himself a dictator in modern civilization" by his control of those indispensable iron highways. Others beside Adams feared the extent of the railroad king's power, and many men to this day have gone through life in the belief that Vanderbilt was an autocrat who said: "The public be damned."

Actually, he said no such thing. His son, William, who inherited the railroad empire, once made the remark to a reporter—and what he meant was that he could not run a non-paying stretch of line as a convenience to "the public," since his first obligation was to his stockholders. In fact, Commodore Vanderbilt himself once told legislative investigators: "I have always served the public to the best of my ability. Why? Because, like every other man, it is my interest to do so." But he did add: "I for one will never go to a court of law when I have got the power to see myself right." In fact, Vanderbilt frequently employed lawyers to fight for him, but his disdainful attitude toward the courts was shared by many men like him. Mem-

bers of the public, in admiring Vanderbilt's wealth, were apt sometimes to forget the manipulations by which it had been achieved.

For the remaining ten years of his life, Vanderbilt supervised the growth of his railroads into a system. In 1868 he attempted to take over his most serious competitor in New York State. This was the Erie Railroad, which started in New Jersey opposite Manhattan, and angled across farmlands all the way to Buffalo. With valuable connections to western cities, the Erie could be a great carrier of coal, flour, meat, and machinery. But its directors in 1868 were ruled by a rascally trio: Daniel Drew, a tobacco-chewing ex-cattle drover who, like Vanderbilt, had invested in steamboats and railroads; fat Jim Fisk, a pleasure-loving one-time peddler; and Jay Gould, a foxy stock market operator. These three used the Erie's treasury to finance various tricky schemes. To raise more money still, they "watered the stock" of the line—that is, sold shares whose total worth was far more than the actual value of the company's property. (Drew was said to have invented this practice when driving cattle to market in New York. He would feed his animals a salty diet, and let them drink until they were bloated just before reaching the slaughterhouse. "Uncle Dan'l" then collected for pounds of "beef" that were only water in an animal's stomach.)

When Vanderbilt tried to buy the controlling interest in the Erie, Drew,

Gould, and Fisk secretly loaded him with shares of bogus stock. When he got the New York courts to issue warrants for their arrest, they fled to New Jersey one dark night and took over a hotel in Jersey City, which they filled with their usual bodyguard of toughs. From this fortress, secure from reprisal, they were able to laugh at Vanderbilt, who had invested millions in purchasing a vast amount of nearly worthless stock. A deal was finally made. The Commodore arranged to let them return to New York and resume operations, and they in turn bought back some of the shares he had acquired. It was Vanderbilt's only defeat.

In a sense, it was not a total loss. Vanderbilt simply set out to make his road better than the Erie. He managed, by 1875, to acquire two additional lines, the Michigan Central and the Lake Shore & Michigan Southern, which gave him a link all the way to Chicago. He then fought aggressively with such rivals as the Erie, the Pennsylvania, and the Baltimore & Ohio. To lure business his way he cut rates to ten cents a bushel on wheat and

Vanderbilt, equipped with a fire hose, has a lead over Fisk and his hand pump as they compete to water railroad stock. This Currier & Ives print was sold during the "Erie War."

25

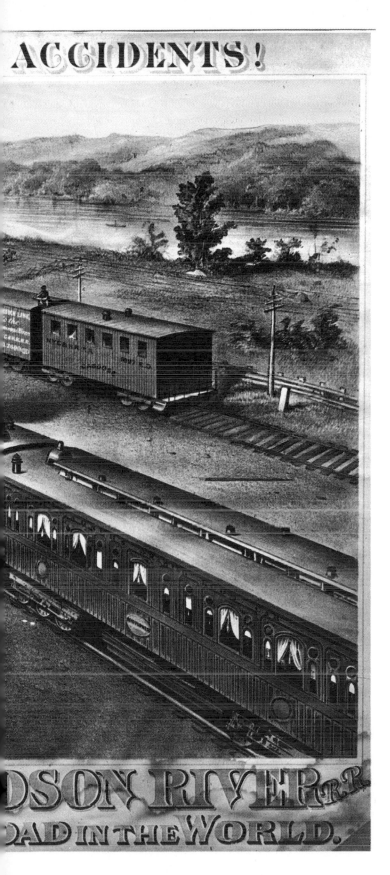

In 1874 the New York Central began a poster campaign to inform the public that it could ride in safety and comfort on "the only four-track railroad in the world." Vanderbilt's basic strategy behind "double-double tracking" the line between Albany and Buffalo, at a cost of nearly $40,000,000, was to combat freight competition from the Pennsylvania Railroad and two other rivals. The investment paid off, with high profits for the Central.

27

thirteen dollars per passenger from Chicago to New York. As one observer put it, the returns would not pay for the axle grease. But such tactics forced the other lines to make agreements with Vanderbilt, which in the end divided traffic and revenues fairly. (Of course, in places where the Central had no competition, rates were not nearly so attractive.)

What was more, the Vanderbilt system was a well-run one. The Commodore, too, watered Central stock to some extent. He believed, however, that the true worth of the company was not in the dollar value of its property, but in its earning promises. And he did his best to make those promises good. In 1871 a brand new terminal for the Harlem Railroad (which was also large enough to house Central, Hudson River, and New York, New Haven & Hartford trains) was opened at New York's Fourth Avenue and 42nd Street. With five acres of space, twelve tracks, and numerous offices and waiting rooms, it was one of the marvels of the period. (The modern Grand Central still stands on this site, and the little avenue cut between 42nd and 47th streets to provide entrances on the west carries Vanderbilt's name to this day.) Soon afterwards, prompted by complaints from New Yorkers who objected to having to wait at street corners until a train had passed by, the tracks were sunk below the level of Fourth Avenue, later renamed Park Avenue, and eventually were covered completely

by pavement and a landscaped area.

The Commodore took the progressive step of four-tracking the Central line from Albany to Buffalo. This meant that two tracks—one in each direction—could be reserved for passenger trains, while two were kept clear for the steadily growing freight traffic. No longer would passengers be delayed by slow-moving strings of boxcars on the rails ahead. Steel rails replaced brittle cast iron. Locomotives lost their gilding and bright brasswork, but grew in speed and hauling power. By 1877 the Central line was hauling Chicago harvesters, Toledo glass, Cleveland petroleum, and countless other products along the margins of Lake Erie and the Mohawk and Hudson valleys. Even in the terrible depression that started in 1873, the Central continued to pay dividends of eight per cent. And workers on the line were understandably bitter when, in 1877, the Central cut their wages on the grounds of "hard times."

As the Commodore grew old, he left much of the business management to his son, William. He mellowed a little, too. Though he had long distrusted book learning, he gave a million dollars to a Methodist university in Nashville, Tennessee, which adopted his name. He joined gentlemen's clubs, played cards with old business friends and enemies, and, after his first wife died in 1868, took a second who was young and pretty. Though father now to one of New York's first families, Vanderbilt con-

The Commodore (center foreground) used the same tactics in racing his trotters on the New York streets as he did in business. "He would drive down the middle of the road," a newspaper recalled when he died, "and intimate to people that they must get out of the way."

tinued to take pride in his own ruggedness. "Here," he once told an overzealous photographer, "don't you rub out the wrinkles and paint me up that way. I ain't particularly pretty, as I know of, but I'm damned if I'll travel in disguise." He would probably have snorted at some of the sentimental editorials and sermons that marked his passing in 1877.

His life had been active, dramatic, and personally rewarding. By the time it was ending, some people had come to think that he represented America even better than statesmen and scientists. The country was dazzled by its new wealth and the men who had made it. Vanderbilt, the richest of them all, made his millions from the power of steam. Other younger men of the same tough grain were already taking different trails to the pot of gold.

29

2
FORTUNES FROM THE FARM

When the United States was still a young country, her greatest wealth lay in millions of acres of rich, virgin soil. At first it could be reached only by cutting down the forest that stretched from the Alleghenies to the Mississippi. But as the tide of expansion swept westward, settlers began cultivating the rolling prairie flatlands that were to become Iowa, Kansas, and Nebraska. In turn, this new territory was cropped and recropped for the grain on which the country's life depended. As the Midwest grew up behind the frontier, mixed farming took over in areas where wheat had been grown. Corn was raised and fed to cattle and hogs, which were moved to centers like Cincinnati to be slaughtered and packed. Farming was becoming an industry, and gradually that industry would develop its own basic essentials: barbed wire for fencing; fertilizer to put life back into the depleted earth; the steel plow to turn the tough prairie sod; the reaper to do the labor of men in the harvest field.

The coming of the Civil War in 1861, with huge armies needing to be fed, brought an even greater stimulus to farming. Cities flowered along with the crops. Somehow food production kept pace with the burgeoning population; and the number of Americans increased from 7,000,000 in 1810 to

The first test of McCormick's reaper, in 1831, dazzled the Virginia gentry, as later shown in a company advertising poster.

31

McCormick was losing a bitter campaign to extend his original reaper patent when he posed for this daguerreotype, in 1848.

almost 63,000,000 when the frontier was officially declared closed in 1890. By developing its agriculture, the United States became a modern nation. Three men with unusual foresight and tenacity found the key to riches in organizing the growth and sale of vast quantities of grain, livestock, and tobacco. In short, they made fortunes from the farm.

Cyrus Hall McCormick was born in 1809. He was the eldest son of a successful farmer in Rockbridge County, in the rolling fertile country of western Virginia. There, men raised wheat, rye, oats, corn, and livestock on small plantations and farms. In a section remote from cities and markets, planters became used to doing things on their own—preaching a sermon, doctoring the sick, or solving a mechanical problem without an engineer's help.

So it was natural for Cyrus' father to tinker with machinery that might help to stretch his limited labor force, and the boy grew up feeling at home in the plantation blacksmith shop. There he watched his father fashion an improved bellows, better machinery for his grist mill, and a device to speed up the process of making hemp fiber into rope. Gradually Cyrus, too, learned to experiment with equipment.

The times called for more and more inventive talent. Farmers were constantly being encouraged to improve the quality and quantity of their crops. Agricultural societies and newspapers, which gave information about new fertilizers and improved seeds were founded. They also offered bounties for any novel gadgets that would speed the age-old tasks of planting a crop, protecting it while it ripened, and gathering it.

In this atmosphere Cyrus turned his thoughts toward better ways of harvesting wheat. This vital crop was still gathered in the ancient fashion, by scything. A first line of men walked through the fields, cutting the stalks of grain with long scythes; and a second line followed them to bind the fallen wheat into sheaves. Six men could cut and bind two or three acres of wheat in a day. But the period when the grain was ready for cutting, yet not overripe, was barely a week or ten days. A machine that could do several men's work would be a godsend to every farmer facing a desperate race with time, and various inventors in Europe and America began experimenting with a number of devices for wheat harvesting.

In the summer of 1831 Cyrus McCormick appeared in a neighbor's field with a home-made machine that successfully combined several previously known principles. It was pulled by one or two horses from the side, so that they would not trample the uncut grain. A main wheel was connected by gears and belts to a revolving reel with sticks set in it, rather like a windmill, and a saw-toothed knife that vibrated back and forth. The reel pressed the grain back against a set of iron fingers that separated the stalks. The knife cut them off, and they fell back on a platform from which they were raked to the ground.

McCormick spent a couple of years perfecting this early reaper, as he named the machine, before he patented it in 1834. It was a homely looking contraption, but with one man driving, one raking, and five following to bind the sheaves, it could cut as many as ten acres a day. It would take nearly three times the number of men to harvest the same ten acres with the scythe.

By the 1860's McCormick's reaper was the small farmer's chief laborer. Here, as one man drives the horses alongside the standing wheat, the reaper cuts the stalks that fall back steadily onto the platform. The man standing on it sweeps them off onto the ground, where the farmer's wife rakes them into bundles. These will later be bound, ready for threshing.

33

McCormick's first Chicago factory is visible just to the right of the steamboat in this 1861 lithograph. After the Chicago fire of 1871 the plant was rebuilt near the city jail, a "standing warning," said a company official, "to clerks and agents to walk uprightly."

Cyrus McCormick saw that his reaper was the seed of a revolution in grain growing. He could have gained a considerable reputation and considerable wealth from selling others the rights to manufacture his invention; but he wanted to do it himself. In 1840 he delivered his first three machines—made in the plantation blacksmith shop—and already he envisioned an army of reapers spreading over the land.

His task was not simple. The Virginia Reaper, as it was now called, had to be sold to American farmers traditionally wary of expensive and untried machinery. And McCormick had many competitors. The toughest was a one-eyed ex-whaler named Obed Hussey, who had patented his own reaper. In 1843 the two agreed to a competitive trial near Richmond. On the first day, McCormick's machine cut seventeen acres, and Hussey's only two. In a second round, the next week, McCormick's cut only twelve but the Hussey reaper broke down altogether. Though Hussey continued in business until 1860, he never produced more than 521 reapers a year,

By the early 1880's, when these metal workers were photographed at their jobs, McCormick was turning out more than 100 farm machines a day. "An angry whirr, a dronish hum, a prolonged whistle, and a panting breath—such is the music of the place," wrote one plant visitor.

while McCormick had leaped ahead and was making thousands. Far more than a mechanically clever farmer, McCormick became a master manufacturer and an aggressive salesman.

In 1847 he made his biggest decision. He set up a reaper factory in the Midwest, in a small settlement of seventeen thousand people at the south end of Lake Michigan. He observed that the little town of Chicago was placed conveniently between the Mississippi River and the Great Lakes; and plans were afoot to use it as a starting point for railroads running westward. Farmers—and reapers—would follow those iron trails to virgin prairies, whose soil, fresh to the plow, could grow many more bushels of wheat per acre than the tired lands to the east. America's "bread basket" of the future would be the northern half of the great table-land between the Mississippi and the Rockies. McCormick foresaw that rail connections would make Chicago the region's capital city, an ideal place to build his machines and his fortune.

His guess was amazingly shrewd. By 1857 Chicago was shipping over nine million bushels of wheat per year from her lake wharves, and her population was approaching one hundred thousand. And in the big brick McCormick works, close to the Chicago River, hundreds of men and steam-driven machines were making four thousand reapers a year.

To sell them, McCormick built up a modern business team. First, he inundated farming counties with advertisements in newspapers and on posters. Then McCormick agents appeared on the scene with sample machines, often entering them against rival reapers in contests at county fairs. Bands tootled, hard cider flowed, and crowds followed the sweating teams, cheering for their favorites. McCormick's machines won most of these contests hands down, and not only in America. In the London Crystal Palace Exhibition of 1851—a World's Fair of its day—the Virginia Reaper won a grand prize. In France, in 1855, a reaper performed for an audience that included the son of Emperor Napoleon III and nine Arab sheiks, and again won the prize. The impressed Emperor bought one. Some reapers even reached Russia.

Once a farmer in Illinois or Iowa had a hankering to buy, McCormick made it easy for him. He could pay one quarter of the cost of a machine worth $100 to $130, and take care of the balance after the harvest was in. With each machine went a sheet of printed instructions and a kit of spare parts. As added protection, however,

36

Above, posing with womenfolk and children in a North Dakota field, farmers proudly display equipment, including a steam-powered thresher, for the 1870 harvest. Below, at nearby Fargo, a horse-drawn float heralds the arrival of McCormick's new twine binder.

McCormick salesmen were trained in repairs, and traveling experts handled unusually complicated breakdowns. Advertising, the installment plan, and factory-trained repairmen were signs of a new age, and they brought impressive results.

Before the Civil War, many Southerners had expected that England would recognize an independent South because of her great need for raw cotton to feed her cloth factories. England *did* need that cotton, but needed still more the 200,000,000 bushels of wheat imported from the North dur-

ing the war years. So, ironically, King Cotton, made prosperous by Yankee Eli Whitney's invention of the cotton gin, was toppled by King Wheat, brought to the throne by the reaper a Virginian had invented.

By 1860 the United States had over 100,000 reapers in use—33,000 of them made by McCormick. That year farmers raised close to 174,000,000 bushels of wheat, mainly in Illinois, Indiana, and Wisconsin. As the increased needs of a wartime economy brought new tracts of land under cultivation, an army of 250,000 reapers and mowers turned out to harvest them. By the early 1870's, McCormick and his rivals were selling 125,000 machines each year.

McCormick grew old and wealthy. He lived comfortably in his elaborate New York and Chicago homes, and was active in the Democratic party and in Presbyterian church affairs. He helped to found McCormick Theological Seminary in Chicago. He still worked hard, much of the time battling other manufacturers who infringed his patents. When he died in 1884, it was estimated that more than half a million McCormick reapers were bringing home the harvest in countries all over the world.

McCormick had a Chicago neighbor who also brought together man's inventiveness, his eternal need for food, and the generous American soil. He was Philip D. Armour, who was born on a farm in Stockbridge, New York in 1832, the year after McCormick first tried out his reaper.

Armour was an adventurous and imaginative youngster. When he was twenty, the great overland trek to the California gold fields was on. He joined a wagon train as a teamster, and made the long march across plain and mountain. In the mining camps he became a contractor, building the sluices—artificial ditches—that carried water from mountain streams to wash the gold-bearing ores out of the earth. After a few years, Armour was six-thousand-dollars richer than when he had arrived, and ready for a triumphant return home to Stockbridge.

But he soon found life on the farm dull and went West again, this time to Milwaukee, where one of his brothers was a wholesale dealer in grain and provisions. By 1862 he was a partner (with John Plankinton) in a firm of his own. Part of its business was buying hogs from local farmers for delivery to slaughterers and packers. The demands of the hungry Union armies created a boom in pork and Armour prospered.

His biggest early success was in a transaction that may seem somewhat sharp, though, in fact, it was quite legal. Toward the end of 1864, when food prices were swollen and seemed likely to stay high as long as the war continued, Armour gambled on his own certainty that the South would shortly be defeated. He contracted to deliver pork in the spring of 1865 at the then-current price of $40 a barrel. He took orders for more meat than he had in his warehouses; he was taking a chance that by the time he had to fulfill his orders, the price would have plummeted. It did. Armour was able to buy pork at $18 per barrel and sell it for $40—and net a profit of some $2,000,000. Disgruntled traders who had to honor their contracts, and buy Armour's meat at twice the market price, had also to agree that here was a young businessman worth watching.

Up till the Civil War the preparation of meat had been a local business. Cattle and hogs were driven in herds to butchers, but could not travel far

"Don't try to get rich too fast, and never feel rich," advised Philip Danforth Armour. At thirty-three he was a multimillionaire.

without serious loss of weight. Once killed, by crude hand methods, their flesh could only be preserved by salting and smoking. Since, even in that form, it could not keep long, each slaughtering center could serve only a small territory.

Armour saw how the railroad network had grown by the war's end. He knew that the great corn belts of Iowa and Nebraska, and the prairie grasses of Kansas and Texas could support hundreds of thousands of hogs and steers. If they could be brought by train to central points like Chicago to be slaughtered in large numbers at high speed; and if the beef and pork could be preserved for rail shipment to the east, then meat packing could be a national industry. Mass production would bring lower prices and bigger markets. Bawling steers

and squealing porkers could build the foundations of fortune in the stockyards. Armour may only have realized all this as time went on, but his moves seem to show a gathering of forces to undertake meat preparation on a massive scale.

In 1875 he moved to Chicago where he was in competition with other aggressive and talented packers, men like Gustavus Swift and Nelson Morris. In fierce battles with each other, they broke through one technical barrier after another. Armour commanded his armies of buyers, workmen, and salesmen from a Chicago office in which he worked from 7 A.M. until late at night. Bald, with reddish side-whiskers, he was a familiar sight in the plant as he checked up on countless small details. He was quick to discharge a workman for a task poorly done. But on the other hand, a good job would be noticed and rewarded with the invitation, "Buy yourself a suit of clothes"—at the boss's expense.

Armour and his rivals began by turning meat packing into an assembly-line operation. Hogs and steers were herded into narrow chutes which led to the slaughterhouses; there they were stunned by a hammer-blow on the head. Next they were slung up by the hind legs to an overhead moving belt. Then they moved past long lines of men working at top speed, who cut their throats, removed their vital organs, peeled off hides and bristles, and sawed the carcasses into chops,

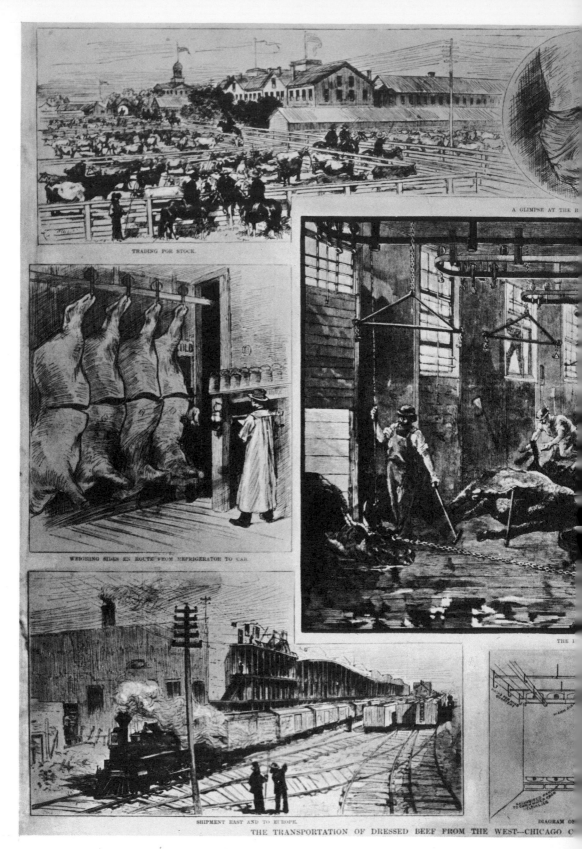

A GLIMPSE AT THE B

TRADING FOR STOCK.

WEIGHING SIDES EN ROUTE FROM REFRIGERATOR TO CAR.

THE I

SHIPMENT EAST AND TO EUROPE.

DIAGRAM OF

THE TRANSPORTATION OF DRESSED BEEF FROM THE WEST—CHICAGO C

A Harper's Weekly *artist sketched the progress of western beef through*

ENGLISH MARKET.

HOW CATTLE ARE SLAUGHTERED.

FRESH MEAT FROM ICE-HOUSE TO CAR.

CAR.

INTERIOR OF REFRIGERATOR CAR.

DS AND SLAUGHTER-HOUSES.—FROM SKETCHES BY THEO. R. DAVIS.

Chicago packing plants and on to eastern markets in refrigerator cars.

steaks, and hams. This organized teamwork could process thousands of animals a day—the product of a hundred farms or an entire ranch. A steer, raised for two years in far-off Texas, driven hundreds of miles by cowboys to Abilene or Dodge City, then shipped further hundreds of miles by cattle car to the Union Stockyards, could be turned into prime beef, ready for the oven, in less than an hour.

Armour's chemists worked out dozens of ways of using what had once been waste products to produce soap, glue, glycerine, and fertilizer. A popular saying had it that every part of the pig was used except the squeal.

Armour and his rival, Gustavus Swift, financed experiments with refrigerator cars. Early models were crude ice chests on wheels, but as time went on, better methods of insulation and of making artificial ice were introduced. Soon Chicago plants were shipping dressed beef and pork to markets thousands of miles away. Since the railroads were reluctant to invest in building such cars, the packers built their own. By 1890 Armour alone had 6,000 refrigerator cars in service. The nation's slaughtering business settled in a few centers linked by rails to the livestock supply—chief among

When this picture of the great Union Stockyards was taken in 1900, Chicago meat packers had the world's largest acreage of stock pens, and processed three million animals a year.

42

them were Kansas City, Cincinnati, and Chicago. Refrigerated ships gave American meat an international market too. By the early twentieth century the poet Carl Sandburg could justifiably address Chicago as "Hog butcher for the world!"

By the end of his twenty-fifth year in Chicago, the New York farm boy had become a meat baron. His investment in banks provided him with money to buy gigantic herds of animals whenever opportunity beckoned. He was a heavy trader in feed grains. His refrigerator cars tied him to the country's railroad empires. He was so much of a success that, in combination with his fellow packers, he could be arbitrary in controlling food prices. He could also deny opportunities in the meat business to thousands of smaller operators. The country was never quite sure how it felt about men like him. Sometimes they were praised as poor boys who had made good. At others they were denounced as wicked monopolists.

No one can set an exact value on the part played by an individual in a great historical development such as the revolution in food-producing techniques. Armour's fortune came partly because of things he had little to do with—the presence of abundant grazing land for vast herds, and the invention of the locomotive to speed cattle and hogs from pasture to slaughterhouse to market. Yet Armour was visibly an organizer of the process that combined invention, natural re-

sources, and capital in order to put food into millions of mouths. This ability won him admiration. He was also rewarded on a princely scale while others who worked desperately hard stayed poor. Such conditions naturally provoked jealousy and raised many questions about the fairness of the new economic order. Both the applause and the criticism were, like Armour and his fortune, characteristic of the new age.

One other fortune came out of American agriculture after the Civil War. It began in a ramshackle barn near Durham, North Carolina, in the lean years after Lee's surrender. The barn belonged to a Confederate veteran named Washington Duke. He had come back from the wars with two blind mules and fifty cents in cash. But he had hope, energy, and three strong sons. Together, they grew a crop of the broad, yellow-leafed tobacco known in North Carolina as bright leaf. They hung it in the barn, cured it over smoky fires, then undertook the arm-wearing job of pulverizing the cured leaves by beating them with flails. They packed the tobacco in barrels, wrestled them into a wagon, and then traveled through the countryside making sales. They slept little and ate less. But they returned with a small profit.

The youngest of these brothers was James Buchanan Duke. When the war ended young "Buck" was only nine years old. But he came to believe that tobacco could bring more than salva-

Tobacco plants were first grown for profit by Virginian colonists in the early 1600's.

tion for defeat: the manufacture and sale of its products on a big enough scale could make a man rich.

Business was always at the top of Buck's mind. By the time he was a teen-ager, his father could afford to send him away to school. The boy chose a business academy in Poughkeepsie, New York. He loved the planning of purchases and sales "better than anything else," he said. After school, he returned home to rejoin the family business and by 1880, though only twenty-four, he was its natural leader. And he was ambitious. A small regular income was available from the sale of Duke's pipe and chewing mixtures, but Buck had his eye on bigger things. His goal was a national market for Duke products.

As was so often the case in this period, a machine gave the answer. A man named James Bonsack had in-

vented a machine for rolling cigarettes. The little paper-covered smokes had been gaining on pipe, cigar, and plug in national popularity ever since the Civil War. They were quick to smoke, handy to carry, and neater than the "chaw" that a century ago polka-dotted streets and buildings with puddles of tobacco juice. However, cigarettes could only be rolled by experts, and those experts were not easy to entice to the communities around Durham where the tobacco grew.

But a Bonsack machine, Duke realized in 1881, could be made to roll 100,000 cigarettes a day, as against the handworker's 2,500. Although its design needed improvement, the machine required no skill to operate, and Duke installed two of them. Over the next three years he worked on increasing output until, by 1884, the machines were turning out 200 cigarettes a minute. Just before production hit its peak, he slashed the price of a pack of cigarettes from ten to five cents. "Tobacco is the poor man's luxury," he said. Soaring sales proved him right, and in 1884 Buck set out to establish a factory in New York.

Duke's passion for business helped him out. Since he felt no need for luxuries, he rented a two-dollar-a-week room and ate at cheap restaurants on the Bowery. He gave his life to the study of other men's smoking habits. It was said that he would pick up discarded cigarette packages on the streets, to see which brands were

Rolling cigarettes by hand (above) was costly and too slow to keep up with the demand. Duke perfected machine rolling in 1884 and trebled cigarette sales in a year.

"I always knew I was going to be rich," remarked James Duke. "As early as I can remember, that idea has been on my mind."

most in favor. These were the ones he had to beat. Though frugal in his personal habits, he spent lavish sums of money on advertising. Pictures of Duke-owned brands of cigarettes appeared on billboards, in magazines, and in theatre programs. He had the notion of enticing customers by putting a color-illustrated card in each pack. At first they carried portraits of famous statesmen; later, pictures of baseball players and stage celebrities catered to more popular tastes.

At the office, where Duke worked a fourteen-hour day, he regularly checked records of sales to every tobacconist on the company's mailing list. If sales fell off, even slightly, salesmen in that district were hounded for an explanation. Clerks were taught that the smallest mistake could be noticed by the owner himself. They learned to hustle. Duke once noticed a group of girl clerks signing forms by hand. One was not keeping up with the others. Her name, it appeared, was Maggie McConichie. "Too long," said Duke. "Change your signature to A. B. Cox." And A. B. Cox it was.

By 1890 all this efficiency was paying off. Duke was manufacturing and selling nearly a billion cigarettes a year under various brand names—half the country's total output. But his dream was bigger still. The boy who had gone barefoot and hungry on a wartime Southern farm intended to control the manufacture and sale of every kind of tobacco in America. Using the profits he had made from cigarettes, he bought an interest in rival firms producing cigars, snuff, plug, and pipe tobacco. Then he prodded them into becoming members of a huge combine called a trust, where the direction of all the member firms lies in the hands of a small group of men. Duke called his trust the American Tobacco Company, and as its president his power was almost unlimited.

American Tobacco became a colossus. It was able to offer bonuses and

A Little Tight.

Whether they pictured ballerinas (above) or baseball heroes, Duke insisted that all his premium cards have masculine appeal. Until the 1920's, a "lady" could not smoke.

During World War I the American Tobacco Company shipped trainloads of Bull Durham —ideal for "smoking out the Kaiser"—to United States troops fighting in France.

rebates, or kickbacks, to dealers who would give its wares extra advertising and display space—or who would boycott rival products altogether. One after another, remaining competitors were forced to sell to American Tobacco. Then Duke moved into other areas, buying factories that made boxes, tinfoil, flavoring, and also buying chains of retail tobacco stores. His aim was always to cut down the sums he had to pay others for furnishing him ingredients or selling his products.

American Tobacco moved on relentlessly. Duke's agents began turning up at tobacco auctions in India, Cuba, Egypt, and Greece, to buy new varieties amid exotic surroundings. Agreements were made with British manufacturers to divide territories all over the world. One factory was even set up in China. Around the world men were smoking American Tobacco cigarettes with many different brand names, and all these sales meant huge profits for Duke's tobacco trust.

For the tobacco farmers of the South, Duke was both a boon and a handicap. The mass market for smoking meant increasing crops. Millions of pounds of tobacco were grown annually, and worn-out valleys in the Carolinas knew the sound of the hoe and wagon wheel once more. But the trust also kept down the prices it paid to the farmers. Naturally, they complained. So did the few manufacturers who had withstood the pressure to join American Tobacco. Objections also were raised by retail tobacconists who claimed that the trust's policies left them little margin for profit, and by many other Americans who believed in free competition. Invoking the Sherman Antitrust Act, which had been passed in 1890, the Supreme Court in 1911 ordered American Tobacco reorganized into a number of independent companies.

James B. Duke kept his interest in most of them and his fortune was undiminished. Like most men raised to work hard, he found it hard to relax. He took few vacations, and spent little time at his residences in London and New York, or on his beautiful farm in New Jersey. Work was his life.

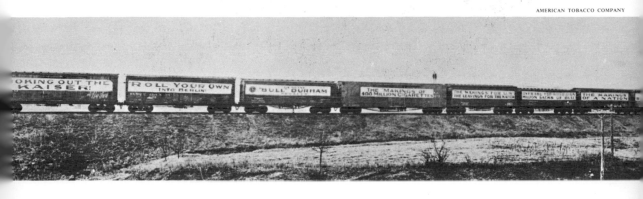

48

When he could no longer expand his empire in smoke, he invested in hydroelectric power developments in North Carolina and Canada. He also invested in people by his gifts. The most notable of them was an endowment of well over $40,000,000, granted to Durham's little Trinity College, which obligingly took the name of Duke University. Forty years after his death in 1925, more people probably associate the name of Duke with this center of higher learning than with tobacco products.

All three of these men who made farmland fortunes were in some ways alike. Originally farm boys, from close-knit families (each began his career in partnership with brothers), they were limited in general education and refinement. Each of them used new techniques of advertising and marketing to build his empire. All three found that their growing wealth pushed them into new lines of work, making them men of great power. This power came directly from the amazing fertility of the American earth. By harnessing the machines of the industrial revolution to create a further revolution in agriculture, which is still going on, these men opened new ways for other adventurers to grow rich from the soil.

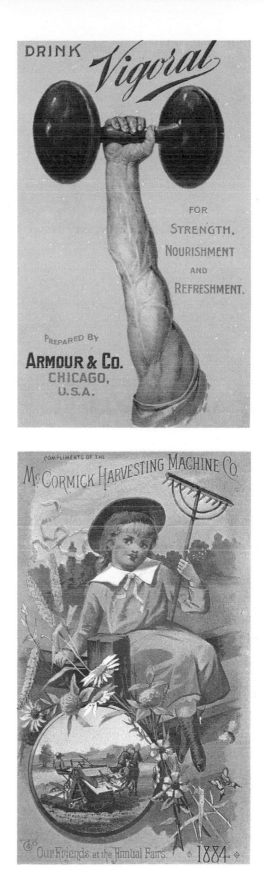

Ingenious advertising made Duke, Armour, and McCormick household words. Vigoral (above), a beef extract, gratified Armour by turning yet another by-product into profits.

3
GOLD OF THE WEST

The great territories of Oregon and California came to the United States by treaty with Britain and by battle on Mexico's plains between 1845 and 1848. The immense work of continental expansion, begun when Jefferson bought the Louisiana country, was complete, and the land of the free stretched from sea to shining sea.

Then the task of exploring and settling these vast regions began. Towering mountains, foaming rivers, dark forests, and treeless prairies seemed to bar the advance westward. They were guarding treasure. Gold, lead, silver, and copper were in the mountains; lumber in the forests; and power in the rivers. A million fat farms slept beneath the prairie grass. The treasure of the West went to those who were brave, lucky, and hard working. It made no difference if the newcomers were rich or poor, or what their manners and accent were. Two American success stories prove this point. The hero of one is a poor Canadian farm boy. The other story is about a wise old Swiss Jew and his seven sons.

James Jerome Hill, the subject of the first story, began his career by not being on time. He arrived in the muddy Mississippi River town of St. Paul, Minnesota, one day in 1856,

With fiery determination James J. Hill drove his Great Northern Railway across two thirds of America. At left is an 1887 construction scene in Montana Territory.

just too late to join a fur-trapping brigade heading westward. Jim was only eighteen, but he had hoped to work his way to the Pacific and take ship to the Orient. Unfortunately, trapping expeditions left only once each year. The young man had to put aside his dream for a while and find work in St. Paul. He was husky and intelligent. His only handicap was one blind eye, destroyed by a badly aimed arrow in a boyhood game of "Indians." However, that did not prevent him from getting a job as a clerk for J. W. Bass and Company, agents for a line of steamboats. Within a year, Jim Hill had forgotten about going to China. He had found more interesting dreams.

Westward of St. Paul stretched the prairie. A few days' journey across it, the Red River flowed north, through the most fertile land in the Minnesota

Hill saw an exciting future in St. Paul, shown above in 1856, the year he arrived in the town formerly known as Pig's Eye. Mississippi River steamboats already operated to downriver towns, but the only method of moving goods to and from the Red River Valley was by slow oxcarts, shown at left assembling for a trip north in 1859. What St. Paul needed, Hill soon decided, was a good railroad.

Territory, into Canada's Manitoba province. Men were already moving into an area that in twenty years' time would be producing the richest wheat harvests in America. And up the Mississippi to St. Paul churned paddlewheelers under columns of smoke, carrying the settlers' needs: dry goods, hardware, furniture, and tools. Jim Hill realized that the job of organizing this traffic was one with great potentialities. The prospects excited him.

Working for various steamboat and railroad companies in St. Paul made Hill a crack transportation agent, with a head full of facts about routes, distances, and costs. In 1865 he went into business for himself. He learned his territory the hard way, personally visiting isolated huts and hamlets where he sold coal, provisions, pumps, and reapers. He forded icy rivers, was stung by hailstorms, and went thirsty in the brassy heat of prairie summers.

He would and could do anything, from assembling a carload of machinery to setting a traveling companion's dislocated arm. When he was thirty-two, he proved to be a fighter who would take on an enemy of any size.

In 1870 there was only one steamboat on the Red River, the *International*, which carried passengers and freight up to the growing Canadian center of Winnipeg. It belonged to the great Hudson's Bay Company, which for two hundred years had acted as Britain's sole trading agent in the Canadian Northwest. It made a great deal of money from its monopoly of the Red River water traffic and was not accustomed to competition. The Hudson's Bay Company governor learned with some surprise that a spanking little boat named the *Selkirk* had suddenly appeared on the river and was giving the *International* stiff competition. The new packet belonged to Jim Hill, whose service and rates were good enough to take a considerable number of dollars out of the Company's pocket. What was more, he had found a law that would bar the foreign boat from American waters. Half angry, half admiring, the Company fought back by transferring the *International* to the control of an American, Norman Kittson. After a brisk rate war, the mighty Company was willing to compromise with the upstart newcomer. The two boats and a wagon service across Minnesota were merged as the Red River Transportation Company.

Jim Hill was looking ahead, however, to something better than wagons to carry the trade between the Red and the Mississippi rivers. The Canadians were planning a rail line from Winnipeg to Pembina, on the Minnesota border. If he could build a connecting link from St. Paul, Jim Hill could tap an endless reservoir of agricultural traffic. But how? There *was* a rickety, unfinished railroad running part way across Minnesota, grandly called the St. Paul & Pacific Railroad. It was, unfortunately, bankrupt. Practically speaking, it belonged to a group of Dutch investors who held its bonds (that is, promises to pay) in return for a loan of some $15,000,000. Since the line was earning nothing, they might be persuaded to sell out for only half that amount. But even that was far more money than Jim Hill could scrape together.

Late in 1877, however, Hill saw the ghost of a chance. The St. Paul & Pacific had been offered a five-million-acre land grant by the Minnesota Legislature on condition that it build about 770 miles of track by the end of 1878. The value of such a huge grant would more than pay back the cost of buying the line, if it could be bought. Hill and his Canadian associates in the Red River Transportation Company put their heads together with bankers they knew. Somehow, Hill and his friends borrowed the money to buy out the Dutch investors, with the sure knowledge that they could never pay off the loan unless the line

Two watercolors by an Austrian artist who visited the Great Lakes in the 1850's give a glimpse of railroad pioneering in the wilderness. Above, surveyors plotting a route across swampland near Lake Huron are ignored by a party of duck hunters, unaware that—since people will settle wherever the railroads go—their sporting days are numbered. Ahead of settlers lured by promises of cheap, fertile land came developers to clear the town sites of the future. Below, a team of surveyors lays out streets deep in the Minnesota forest.

was finished in time to claim the grant.

Jim Hill became a dynamo of activity in 1878. He got together rails and equipment on credit. He hustled to the offices of a rival line in the Northwest, the Northern Pacific, and bluffed them out of building their own connection to Winnipeg. He roared in and out of his St. Paul office, hiring work gangs and arranging to ship supplies out to the point where the tracks were inching westward. From time to time, he supervised rail laying operations personally. The men worked desperately to bridge rivers and cut through hills, tormented first by summer heat, dust, and flies, and then by winter blizzards that froze their hands to their iron tools. But James J. Hill drove them on, and legend has it that he sometimes stripped off his coat to swing a pick himself, his beard whipping in the chill winds, and his one good eye glowing like a live coal.

By January, 1879, the line was complete from St. Paul to Winnipeg. The land grant, now earned, was a future asset worth millions in itself. By 1881, at an average price of five dollars an acre, land sales were bringing in $100,000 a month to Hill's treasury. And, as he had expected, a golden flood of grain poured over the rails of the St. Paul & Pacific, now reorganized and renamed the St. Paul, Minneapolis & Manitoba Railroad.

Destiny works in curious ways. As a boy, Jim Hill came to St. Paul in hopes of going to the Pacific coast

This poster, distributed in 1904, announced "greatly reduced one-way colonist rates" to induce easterners and immigrants to journey west and settle down along Hill's railroad.

with fur-trappers. Because he missed that chance, he entered the field of transportation, and by following his opportunities, finally became a railroad builder. In a sense, he could take up his trek toward the Pacific once more by extending his railroad westward. In 1879 the territory that would soon become the Dakotas, Montana, Idaho, and Washington contained, in a cynic's words, nothing but buffalo bones. Yet Hill knew the region was potentially an empire of gold, lumber, cattle, and wheat. He began to create the well-built railroad line that could turn his dream into a reality.

From 1879 to 1893 he added trackage to his original line. This time he was in no hurry. Each section was carefully surveyed and graded, and from the main line he ran off many little spurs to places that would one day be mines, ranches, and farming communities. In 1890 Hill's various links of track were united in the Great Northern railroad system. In 1893 he reached the Pacific coast at Seattle.

Ten years earlier, another northern transcontinental line had been completed, the Northern Pacific. It had been built in a hurry, to get a sizable land grant. Various promoters had successively bought and bankrupted it. Hill waited until 1893, when a big depression toppled the Northern Pacific's shaky financial structure. Then he bought control of it. Later, in 1901, through an alliance made with the great banking house of J. P. Morgan, he raised money to buy stock

that divided control of the Chicago, Burlington & Quincy line between the Great Northern and the Northern Pacific railroads. The Burlington linked Hill with Chicago, St. Louis, Omaha, and Denver. The rising cities of the great West joined his empire.

He ran the empire on the basis of long-range planning. To populate the area through which the Great Northern ran, he fixed special passenger rates, aimed particularly at the nearly nine million immigrants who flooded into the country between 1880 and 1900. A newcomer to the Northwest could get help from the Great Northern in picking out a government homestead in, say, Montana and could ride to it for ten dollars. The Great Northern set up farms on which scientific experts developed fresh varieties of seed and then distributed it free to farmers. Hill would get his money back many times over when the new farmers' grain came to his railroad sidings for shipment east.

But Hill did not rely solely on the trade in farm products. He bought coal and iron lands and offered them to interested mining companies at bargain rates. Then he watched the profits roll in as gondola cars full of ore and anthracite clicked over the rails to St. Paul and Duluth. By cutting the rate on western fir and pine from ninety to forty cents per hundred pounds delivered to Chicago, he forced southern pine into second place in Midwestern lumber yards.

In addition, he wanted to make sure

Hill built two of the largest cargo ships in the world to carry goods to and from the Far East by connecting with a special train, the Oriental Limited, at the Seattle dockside. All three appear in this 1905 photograph.

that his freight cars did not travel back empty from their eastern unloading points. He negotiated with Japanese and Chinese businessmen, and offered to carry American steel, oil, cotton, and flour to the Pacific coast for them at rates that cut out his European competitors. To pick up trade with the Orient at the dockside, where the Great Northern tracks ended, Hill created the Great Northern Steamship Company with two ships, the *Minnesota* and the *Dakota*. With ships docking in Yokohama and Hong Kong, and his agents in Germany, Norway, and Sweden persuading farmers to move to Minnesota, Hill's operations had become truly international.

Like all emperors, Hill was eventually challenged. In 1901 his hold on the rail traffic of the Northwest came under the jealous eye of Edward H.

Harriman, a powerful New York stockbroker. By skillful stock purchases, Harriman had gained control of the Union Pacific Railroad, which had important branches in Idaho and Oregon. He did not intend to share the wealth of these regions with Hill's Great Northern.

Just after Hill bought the Burlington line in 1901, Harriman quietly began to place orders for shares of Northern Pacific. If he got enough of them, he could break his rival's grip on that line. When the word leaked out to Hill, he too began to buy. As the millionaires fought, the price of Northern Pacific shares climbed dizzily. In desperation brokers who had

58

contracted to deliver the stock sold other holdings in order to cover themselves, and a near-panic ensued. Meantime the public grumbled about a war between rich men that threatened to ruin banks and start a new business depression. At last a compromise was reached, with Harriman getting representatives on the Northern Pacific board, but Hill staying in control.

Hill and Harriman then hatched a plan to create a huge holding company, the Northern Securities Company, that would consolidate all their subsidiaries: the Great Northern, the Northern Pacific, and the Burlington. But this monster railroad monopoly aroused the country's anger and was eventually attacked by the United States Government, which sued to dissolve it under the Sherman Antitrust Act. In 1904 the Supreme Court gave it the death blow. Hill and Harriman kept heavy individual holdings of stock in the three lines. The Great Northern and the Union Pacific continued to battle each other for business in Oregon for a long time after the Northern Securities case. In fact, they were still doing so after Harriman died in 1909 and Hill in 1916.

Toward the end of his life, Jim Hill had many of the things that rich men of his time liked to display. He owned homes in New York and St. Paul, and he had a fine collection of French paintings to show that he was no mere frontier roughneck. He spent little time looking at them, however. Like most men of his kind he remained

Hill's shaggy grimness and his iron-fisted tactics caused an unknown wag to compose the line: "Twixt Hill and Hell, there's just one letter, Were Hill in Hell, we'd feel much better." This photograph was taken in 1900.

deeply absorbed in work, with occasional time out to pay attention to his family of ten children.

As he grew old, Hill was courted for his wealth and feared for his still-hot temper. He was condemned by many as a monopolist who got an unjust share of the wealth sweated from the country by loggers, mine workers, and farmers. Others pointed out that without his driving, scheming, and maneuvering, the wealth of the West would never have been unlocked. There is some truth in both viewpoints, and most people would agree that James J. Hill was indeed a giant-sized figure, well fashioned to match the greatness of the West.

Immigrants bid farewell to their homeland upon embarking for America—a familiar European scene after the 1830's.

The second story of Western adventure started in Switzerland in 1847. A Jewish tailor named Simon Guggenheim decided that America offered his family a wonderful chance for success and freedom. Like millions of other immigrants, he sailed from a European port with his family including a son of nineteen named Meyer.

The family settled in Philadelphia, where Simon felt confident his boy could build himself a future. Few men had their hopes so thoroughly gratified. For Meyer Guggenheim had a shrewdness, a knowledge of what he wanted and how to get it, and a firm character that bespoke leadership. He was the kind of purposeful person who could do wonders with an opportunity, and the move to America gave him just that. In Switzerland, as a Jew, he would probably have found social and economic advancement closed to him by age-old tradition. Across the Atlantic it was different.

Even in abundant America, Meyer had to work hard for a living. He found employment doing what many of his fellow Philadelphian Jews had done before him. With a sack on his back, he trudged from door to door, peddling laces, needles, ribbons, and knickknacks. It was slow and discouraging work. One day it occurred to Meyer that the manufacturer of the articles in his peddler's pack had an easier route to success. He took a can of stove polish from his stock and had a chemist analyze it for him. Then, with a few dollars of carefully hoarded

60

family savings, he and his father began to make it themselves. The difference in the profit they received on a ten-cent can of polish was small. But the extra nickels, prudently saved, made it possible for Meyer Guggenheim, as he grew older, to become more than a footsore salesman.

Meyer's ideas did not end with becoming a stove-polish maker. For him, one business success was simply a steppingstone to another—each profitable deal gave him the resources to satisfy a teasing little inner voice that said, "There are better things. Try them." The earnings from polish went into a succession of other business operations—wholesaling cloth, spices, coffee, and lace. As Meyer's enterprises prospered, he married a girl he had met on the voyage from Europe, and moved with her into a succession of homes, each one a little larger, a little finer, and in a more elegant Philadelphia neighborhood. This was fortunate because, after 1854, children kept adding to his pleasures and responsibilities—eleven in all. Eight were boys, one of whom died in childhood. For the others—Isaac, Daniel, Murry, Solomon, Benjamin, Simon, and William—he had formed definite plans.

Meyer Guggenheim was a strict but loving father. His sons were set to work early learning the ways of the business world. Education was, for them, a preparation for future usefulness in the family company, M. Guggenheim's Sons, which Meyer created

A peddler shows his wares to a spellbound family. These nineteenth-century door-to-door salesmen brought news as well as daily household needs to isolated communities.

in 1881. Dan, for example, was sent to school in Switzerland, where he could learn something of foreign languages and manners and, naturally, meet people important to his father's lace-importing business who would initiate him into the tricks of the trade. From their patriarchal father the sons inherited a love of business affairs and an ability to initiate and manage imaginative ventures in the economic world. As they grew older, they continued to live near him, to raise their families in close proximity to his, and share their work with him right up to his death. All became successful businessmen themselves.

In 1881 Meyer took the step that

Up a tortuous, 13,000-foot-high trail struggle some of the miners who hoped to cash in on the rich silver and lead deposits discovered at Leadville, Colorado, in 1877. Meyer Guggenheim reached the town in 1881, upset by the journey and afraid that he had invested $5,000 unwisely. "What a place," he muttered to his partner, Charles Graham. "God help you if there is no million dollars in that mine."

determined the basic course of the family fortunes: he turned from merchandise to metals. It began one day when he suddenly appeared in the rip-roaring mining town of Leadville, Colorado. In his sober eastern clothing, with his long whiskers neatly parted in the middle, he looked out of place among the grizzled prospectors of the Rockies. He may even have felt foolish, for an indulgence in the habit of taking risks on unusual prop-

ositions had brought him two thirds of the way across America to look at —a hole in the ground!

As he became wealthier, Meyer liked to invest his money here and there—a few railroad stocks, for example, or a loan at good interest. One day, a man named Charles Graham came to Guggenheim to ask for money to help develop a couple of silver mines that he had bought for a song from an out-of-luck miner. Meyer offered, instead, to go into partnership. He had an inkling that a mine was a useful property and would go on producing wealth no matter whether stocks went up or down. When he first saw the "A.Y." and the "Minnie," however, on a wet and chilly day in Leadville, his heart sank. They were filled with water; and many thousands of dollars would be needed for pumps and repairs before they could be productive.

Many times in the next few years Meyer wondered if his judgment had been wise. But slowly, the yield from the mines began to catch up with the expenses of running them. Then, suddenly, output skyrocketed. By 1889 more than a million dollars' worth of silver and lead had been taken from the mines. Meyer Guggenheim had become what the Western newspapers called a bonanza king.

For someone else that might have been enough. However, Meyer Guggenheim planned further. His few years of mining experience convinced him that the big profits were made by smelters and refiners who, in their gigantic plants, turned ore into finished metal. In 1887 he made three breathtaking decisions. First, he would build his own smelting and refining plant. Second, he would gradually shift his total investments into the mining industry. Third, the smelting company would be a family affair with each of the brothers taking a full part.

Meyer was the kind of father whom sons obeyed. It turned out, too, that he was right in his impulsive idea that the hidden metals of the Rockies would make the whole family's fortune. In 1888 the Philadelphia Smelting and Refining Company opened a $1,250,000 smelter in Pueblo, Colorado. Dan became the eastern head of the company; Murry, its president, organized more financial connections in the West. Isaac was busy winding

Some 40,000 people had flocked into Leadville by 1880 to find that like all mining camps it offered few beds and charged astronomical prices. A magazine artist showed weary latecomers bedding down on a saloon floor.

At the boom's height in 1880, Leadville's main street sported an array of false-front businesses, including a bookshop with a striped awning (right). From an office on this street, Guggenheim was sent the jubilant telegram: "Struck rich ore in A.Y. You have a bonanza."

64

up the lace business, while Simon was hunting for new mines to furnish ore for the smelter. Ben was general manager at Pueblo, and Will was studying metallurgy so that he could do his part. They all worked and they all prospered. Before too long, they began to look beyond the boundaries of the United States.

Mexican ores could be dug, carried, and refined very cheaply. So in the 1890's Dan and Murry Guggenheim went to Mexico City to conduct negotiations with the government of dictator Porfirio Díaz. Their Spanish was excellent, and their European manners most acceptable to Latin-American gentlemen. Soon they had permission to build two smelters in Mexico.

There were unusual problems, of course. One of their engineers was slashed to death in his bunk by bandits. Mexican laborers could only be coaxed into sticking to the job by the promise of a rent-free house for twenty-five days' work per month. But the smelters were built, and new mines were located and bought. When other American smelters were paying high prices for ore, the Guggenheims were cutting costs and piling up profits. By 1895 they were estimated to be earning over $1,000,000 a year.

Toward the end of the century, they showed just how good they had become in the boom-and-bust mining and refining game. A group of promoters decided to organize a smelters' trust that would dictate prices to the country's miners. They included some shrewd and well-financed operators. One of them, Henry H. Rogers, was a partner in Standard Oil, who had already organized a copper-mining monopoly worth $75,000,000 in stock. The smelting combine was set up as the American Smelting and Refining Company, and it moved boldly to buy up every smelting plant in the country. Its agents offered old Meyer Guggenheim $11,000,000 for his mines, his smelters, and his newly built copper refinery in Perth Amboy, New Jersey. Guggenheim laughed. He wanted no part of $11,000,000 in the stocks of a new company. "Who knows what good their stock is?" he told his boys. The American Smelting and Refining Company thereupon set to work to run the Guggenheims out of business.

They were in for a surprise. Meyer and Dan Guggenheim fought back with extraordinary shrewdness. They contracted with independent mine owners whose small outputs were spurned by the mighty American Smelting monopoly. They paid top prices for the ores that fed their smelters. Mining men found it profitable to do business with the Guggenheims. Meyer and Dan undersold the trust in the lead market, and made deals with the mineworkers' union that enabled Guggenheim plants to operate while those belonging to the trust were paralyzed by strikes.

In 1901 Goliath gave in to David. M. Guggenheim's Sons were taken into the trust, not on Rogers' terms, but on their own. And their terms included virtual control of the organization. Dan was made chairman of a board of directors that included four of his brothers.

The Guggenheims' key move in the trust war was the organization, in 1899, of the Guggenheim Exploration Company. Known as Guggenex, it hired the best engineering talent in the world to develop supplies of ores outside the United States, where no rival could threaten to take them over. In the years before the First World War, the brothers used Guggenex to explore and develop mines of all sorts—tin in Bolivia, gold in Alaska, diamonds in Africa. Perhaps the most interesting part of their change from silver kings to smelter millionaires, and then to general overlords of world mining, was their move into the field of copper.

This metal had a romantic history in America. In the 1840's valuable copper deposits had been discovered in Michigan's upper peninsula, an inhospitable hard-to-reach region, not far removed from its Indian past. Thousands of tough miners swarmed into the area. By 1880 nearly thirty thousand tons a year were being shipped out across Lake Superior. The demands of modern industry—and especially of the electrical age—swelled the market further and intensified the search for new mines. Men grubbed for copper in Arizona's Apache country, and made the fortunes of giant combines like the Anaconda Copper

Mining Company in Butte, Montana. By 1895 the United States was producing more than half the world's copper output.

The Guggenheims followed this adventurous pattern of expansion as they shifted their interests. In 1906 they began building a $20,000,000 railroad to develop the Kennecott mine in Alaska. By the next year they were opening mines in far away Chile.

The Guggenheims' empire was worldwide and their power formidable. In 1909 the extension of their Alaskan ventures to include a coal field worth $25,000,000, in direct violation of government conservation policies, involved the family in a national scandal. A congressional investigation acquitted the Secretary of the Interior of being an agent for the Guggenheims, but the case considerably tarnished their reputation.

Meyer Guggenheim lived out his last years enjoying the opera, horses, good cigars, and the company of an increasing horde of grandchildren. It must sometimes have amazed him

This smelting plant at Leadville was absorbed into the Guggenheim empire after the company gained its victory over the American Smelting trust in 1901. Smelters separated valuable metals from raw mine-ores; firms controlling them in effect controlled the mining industry.

67

to think that all but two of his sons were multimillionaires. Two years after his death in 1905, the total stock value of the Guggenheim enterprises was estimated at more than two hundred million dollars.

Meyer Guggenheim's sons spent their money to enrich their country as well as themselves. Daniel created a foundation that invested millions in aviation research. Murry endowed a free dental clinic. Simon instituted the series of fellowships and grants that allow artists, writers, scholars, and scientists a year or more of free time for creative work. His wife has additionally benefited New Yorkers by generously endowing the Museum of Modern Art. And in 1959 Solomon Guggenheim gave the city a new landmark, a museum that bears his name and houses his own collection of modern art, in a striking circular building on Fifth Avenue designed by famed architect Frank Lloyd Wright.

The gift of the West to Meyer Guggenheim was a shower of mineral wealth. The secret of his success was having seven sons who combined business ability with complete loyalty, enabling him to expand what initially was a family business into an enormous enterprise run on a global scale.

Posing beneath the portrait of grandfather Simon Guggenheim are, left to right, Benjamin, Murry, and Isaac; their father Meyer; then Daniel, Solomon, Simon, and William.

In this 1906 cartoon a highly successful Rockefeller has stripped the suit off a famous American (visible on a back seat in his underwear) and poses in his place as "Uncle John." Unflatteringly perched on an oil can is Senator Nelson W. Aldrich, his staunch supporter.

70

4

KING OF THE OIL INDUSTRY

The biggest business success story of the nineteenth century began in 1859 in the little Pennsylvania town of Titusville. There, a former railroad conductor and hotel clerk named Edwin L. Drake drilled the first successful oil well. Science had just discovered that petroleum was potentially much more than a thick, smelly black liquid sometimes used in patent medicines. Benjamin Silliman, a famous chemist on the faculty at Yale, had pointed out that refined oil yielded many possibly valuable products. Lubricating grease for machinery, kerosene for lamps, and paraffin for waterproofing were only a few of them. Petroleum was really liquid gold. When Drake showed how it could be extracted by drilling, instead of being laboriously scooped out of pools of seepage from the earth, an invasion like the gold rush began. By 1861 the Titusville area was packed with oil derricks, shanties, tents, and saloons. Workmen in grease-blackened clothes jostled promoters and bankers in top hats on every street. Men grew rich, or went broke overnight, as the big boom in oil roared on.

News of the oil region's progress was reported in newspapers across the country. In Cleveland, Ohio, the accounts were read by a successful young businessman doing well in wartime trade as a partner in the wholesaling firm of Clark and Rockefeller. But John D. Rockefeller craved something bigger. The oil industry attracted him. It was like a crude, powerful giant, able to make an emperor out of a man clever enough to become its master. Rockefeller was convinced that he was such a man.

Though still only in his twenties, Rockefeller had already learned a good deal about discipline and hard work. He was born in 1839 on a New York farm. His father was a man of miscellaneous and nondescript occupations who traded in salt, lumber, and horses, and later sold herbal medicines. He taught his three sons to enjoy bargaining and to get the most possible from it. John's mother emphasized the virtues of working hard and saving money. A strict Baptist herself, she brought up her children to believe that whatever they owned came from the Lord. A tenth, or tithe, must always be paid back to Him in charitable gifts.

Young John worked hard and soon learned to make and save money. One of his first ventures consisted of finding out where a hen turkey was hiding her eggs. If he did so, he was promised, he might raise and sell the chicks. John concealed himself in the tall weeds near the barnyard and spied on the lady gobbler, until he tracked her to her nest. The money he earned was carefully put away in a blue china crock. Later on, his extra farm jobs helped to fill the crock. Then one day he lent a neighboring farmer $50, and received it back, in due time, with $3.50 in interest. He had learned to let money work for him, even as he was working for money.

The family moved to Cleveland in 1853. John went to high school and then to a business school. He found that he liked commercial subjects, and especially bookkeeping. He was quiet and reserved, and one of his sisters was sure that he was thinking of ways to get ahead. If it ever rained porridge,

Oil booms often turned rural scenes like the one above, with derricks looming on the horizon, into towns like Red Hot, Pennsylvania, below, deserted once its wells ran dry.

she said, John's dish would be sure to be right side up. Soon after completing his studies, he found a job with a firm of merchants where he kept books and did other chores for $3.50 a week. So frugal was he in his habits that within four years he had saved up enough to go into business on his own with Maurice Clark. But even from his tiny starting salary he regularly set aside at least a tenth to give to what he felt were deserving causes. He supported various organizations trying to improve the lot of the Negro, and made regular donations to Catholic charities as well as to the funds of the Baptist church that he faithfully attended.

In 1863 Rockefeller began his close study of the oil business. At the time, oil was more of a game than a business—and a very risky one. Just a few lucky finds by "wildcat" drillers would bring a flood of oil out to mar-

The serious young Rockefeller was already a respected Cleveland businessman when, in 1863, he started his oil refining firm.

ket and prices would tumble. Then there might be a spectacular fire that would wipe out a few wells, or some trouble would develop over hauling barrels of oil to the rail depots. The result would be a shortage of oil and prices would rocket overnight. The railroads that ran into the fields were competing frantically for the freight, and their rates bounced up and down wildly. One day it would be cheapest to ship oil to Pittsburgh, the next day to New York, and the day after to Cleveland. Long-range planning was impossible. Oil refining, Rockefeller learned, was an easy business to get

into—equipment cost little. But it was also easy to lose one's shirt.

Rockefeller was no gambler, yet he found a friend who possessed some capital and was skillful in chemistry and mechanics. John D. induced this man—Sam Andrews—to join him, Maurice Clark, and Clark's two brothers in starting a refinery. Why did Rockefeller take the plunge? Because he could, in the words of an associate, "see farther ahead than anybody else and then around a corner." The market for oil products would be as limitless as a growing country's needs.

Cleveland, close to the oil fields and with good rail and water connections to the industrial markets, was an ideal refining center. Oil had a future in Cleveland, if it could be put on a sound business basis. This would mean stabilizing prices, transportation rates, and output. To tame the wildcat, competition would have to be controlled or eliminated. Some company would have to seize leadership by superior strength and organization; and keep that leadership by constantly exerting pressure on other refineries, or absorbing them if necessary. This became Rockefeller's long-term goal. His initial objective, in 1863, was the conquest of Cleveland; it took him nine years.

He began by a hard-driving campaign to become the best refiner in the city. This involved heavy borrowing. Cleveland bankers were willing to deal with the pious and persuasive

Mr. Rockefeller, and he used their money to expand. He bought a second plant, built warehouses, gathered in tankers and wagons, started the manufacture of barrels, and even bought timber lands to guarantee a supply of wood. The Clark brothers, who lacked the nerve for big-time investing, were soon persuaded to sell out their share of the business. Rockefeller brought his own brother, William, into the firm (renamed Rockefeller and Andrews) and sent him to New York to look for foreign customers. But still

By the time this picture of Standard's first refinery was taken in 1870, Rockefeller had been in business seven years and controlled one tenth of the country's refining industry.

more money was needed. In 1867 Rockefeller invited into the company Henry M. Flagler, a wealthy Cleveland merchant as hardheaded as John D. himself. Other investors were attracted, and by 1870 Rockefeller felt it was time to incorporate his business and sell shares of stock to raise the capital. The Standard Oil Company of Ohio was created, and ten thousand shares were offered at $100 each.

By that time, Rockefeller's tight control of the business of making and selling refined oil—from the well to the customer—was already showing impressive results. As early as 1865, Rockefeller and Andrews were refining 500 barrels a day, more than any of the thirty other Cleveland refineries. By 1870 the figure was up to 3,000 a day, an amount that gave Rockefeller the chance to make his biggest move up to then.

First he went to the Lake Shore Railroad (controlled by Vanderbilt's New York Central) and promised to give up shipping oil products by water, and to provide sixty railroad carloads daily, in return for considerable rate reductions by the Central-Lake Shore management. This gave the railroad the advantage of regular oil traffic, and gave Rockefeller an extra edge on other shippers of refined oil. Next, he entered another railroad deal—this one devised not by himself but by a railroad president and carried out in the utmost secrecy. (Rockefeller did not disapprove the principle of the arrangement; he considered it too limited in scope.) Under this plan, Standard and several other leading Cleveland refineries would agree to divide up all their traffic evenly among the three main railroads serving the city—the Pennsylvania, the Erie, and the Central. In return, the refiners' combination (chartered as the South Improvement Company) would receive rebates, or kickbacks, on the freight rates charged for their oil—*and also on oil shipped by refiners outside the combination.* In addition, member firms in the South Improvement Company would receive information on all shipments of their business enemies. Those not in the combine would be hard put to survive.

Such arrangements have a basic unfairness about them, given our present belief that railroads, as common carriers, should deal equally with all customers. But railroading is also a business, and in the 1870's it was a savagely competitive business. The roads themselves welcomed, and often initiated, such arrangements to even traffic by rewarding, with rebates, those who would agree to furnish regular shipments. As one railroad man put it in testimony before a Senate committee, "A man may say, 'I can give you so much business.' If you can depend on that you may make definite arrangements accordingly." Railroaders got the blessings of regular planning from such "evener pacts"—and were not concerned about the disadvantages experienced by shippers who were not participants in them.

As it happened, news of the South Improvement Company plan leaked out. There was such public outrage and fury at the prospect of a big refiners' pool squeezing out smaller independent firms that the plan was dropped. Rockefeller now visited other Cleveland refiners, and pointed out what a tremendous advantage they would have had in dealing with railroads and crude oil producers if they had stuck to their combination. Why not get that advantage anyway, he suggested, even if the South Im-

As early as 1853 Cleveland was a thriving port with docks on Lake Erie (left) and the Cuyahoga River (foreground), and a canal link (right) leading to the busy Ohio River.

provement Company was dead? Why not simply join up with Standard?

One after another, thirty-two independent refiners sold out to Rockefeller for Standard stock or cash. They were faced with a straightforward choice: sell out or be driven out by this intense young man with the reddish side-whiskers and the calculating eyes. They chose to be rich Standard stockholders and directors, rather than bankrupt independents.

At thirty-three, Rockefeller was king of Cleveland's petroleum products industry. It was time for his next campaign. This consisted of applying the techniques he had used in conquering Cleveland to conquer the country at large. Standard would have to lead the nation as it had led the city on Lake Erie. Rockefeller's son, John D., Jr., later observed that the American Beauty rose could be produced in all its loveliness "only by sacrificing

A misguided remark by John D. Rockefeller, Jr. was made-to-order copy for the nation's cartoonists. Here, his father clips one more competitive bud from the Standard rose.

the early buds which grew up around it." To his father, competing firms were the early buds of a national refining industry. They must fall before the pruning knife. Rockefeller argued that this was merely "a law of nature and a law of God."

Other businessmen were not impressed with this argument. They contended that Standard (later to become a synonym in the popular mind for Rockefeller) continually violated all the rules of business fair play. In return, company spokesmen insisted that their success was "the result of the application of better methods and of better business principles than have been brought against us." There was truth in both statements.

Rockefeller was indeed a master businessman. He could make and carry out plans that involved whole countries, and millions of dollars, and years of work. During the 1880's the company bought oil fields, built tanks and warehouses all over the country, and set up sales agencies on every continent. Lamps in Peru and in Egypt, in Peking and in Bombay, burned Standard-made kerosene. Yet at the same time, Rockefeller kept the smallest details in view. Instructions would come from the front office to seal a tin can with two drops less of solder. A barrel factory superintendent once received a letter from Rockefeller himself—the head of a corporation earning millions a year—concerning barrel stoppers: "Your March inventory showed 10,750 bungs on hand. The report for April shows 20,000 bungs bought, 24,000 used, and 6,000 bungs on hand. What became of the other 750?" The barrel bungs were worth a fraction of a cent apiece. But Rockefeller realized that these tiny economies, multiplied by an output of hundreds of thousands of barrels, totaled millions in savings over the years.

Rockefeller was now the country's biggest buyer of crude oil, and he used his power to control the price of the "black gold." Standard could stockpile petroleum in its warehouses and

Petroleum, which began the nineteenth century as a patent medicine, ended it as a major source of light, heat, and power. In 1865 one oil firm advertised the new "black gold" by commissioning a set of dances in its honor.

hold it there for a while without purchasing new supplies. During such a period, the price of crude oil would naturally fall. Financially weak operators would be forced out of the drilling business—sacrificed to Rockefeller's desire to achieve an efficient oil industry, without overproduction, whatever the cost in human terms.

A number of producers who resented Standard's highhanded methods finally decided to fight back. In 1878 they began building the Tidewater pipeline to pump cheap oil to the Atlantic coast. (By the mid 1870's pipelines were carrying increasing amounts of the country's output of crude oil to refineries there.) The producers' group hoped that their action would encourage other refiners to enter the field and challenge Standard. But Rockefeller moved fast to expand his own pipeline system and buy up possible purchasers of Tidewater oil.

The men behind Tidewater Pipe pumped their first oil across the Alleghenies in 1879 with wild hopes of success. But before long they found that their market in the East could not expand as they had intended because the storage tanks, railroad cars, and refining space they needed already belonged to Rockefeller. They managed to extend their pipeline to the eastern seaboard, but their threat to Standard's domination of the industry was no longer serious. In 1883 the two companies signed a contract dividing the eastern outflow from the Pennsylvania oilfields: Tidewater's share was 11.5 per cent; Standard's was 88.5—a lion's portion. Another competitor had been "stabilized" by Rockefeller.

Oil retailers as well as producers speedily learned to cooperate. If they traded with other refiners, their shipments of Standard products suddenly stopped. Disappointed customers were likely to find Standard kerosene being sold in a new store across the street—at lower prices than before. Nor could the retailers buy other brands in secret, for Standard had agents working in railroad offices who traced every shipment of "enemy" oil products down to the last storekeeper's counter. It was even charged that Rockefeller's men dealt with competing refineries by stirring up labor trouble, or by bribing an engineer to jam the machinery.

By 1886 Rockefeller's firm was the

Before the tank car was invented in 1865, crude oil usually traveled from well to refinery in barrels loaded onto railroad flatcars, such as those at left. After 1870 a network of pipelines began to crisscross the country, laid by the slow hand-methods pictured above.

overlord of a great and essential national industry. It controlled about 85 per cent of the country's oil refining and marketing business. Its output was over ten million barrels annually, and earnings from all branches of its business totaled over $15,000,000. In order to coordinate the work of various producing, shipping, and marketing companies under the Standard flag, the company lawyers had incorporated them into a trust, a word that came to mean, in the public's view, the same thing as a monopoly.

There was an understandable wave of critical reaction. Standard had such enormous power! Anyone who chose to manufacture oil and its by-products, or to move them, or to sell them —whether he was a railroad president or a corner grocer—discovered that this single concern set the terms on which he could do business. It was almost impossible to fight back. Standard could afford to hire the best lawyers in the country to defend its interests in the courts. In addition, the giant corporation could easily exert influence on many politicians and editors who presented its case to the public in legislatures and in the press.

In time, Standard became an enemy, not only to those who suffered under its control, but to everyone who felt that such an economic giant had no place in America—where freedom of opportunity and equality of treatment were basic values. The great oil trust seemed the prize example of the new giant organization—frighteningly efficient, terrifyingly strong. Farmers' organizations; labor unions; and reformers in general, concerned about the power of business, joined in decrying Rockefeller's organization. In 1894 a crusading journalist, Henry Demarest Lloyd, wrote an angry book, *Wealth Against Commonwealth*, denouncing sins the trusts committed against democracy. He devoted most of it to an assault on Standard Oil.

For most people, John D. Rockefeller, Sr. was the visible symbol of the Standard trust. Actually, he shared the direction of affairs with many able lieutenants. Since 1876 he had been doing more and more business from New York. In 1884 the trust set up a new company headquarters in the country's business capital. From a building at No. 26 Broadway, in the financial district, Rockefeller and his co-directors undertook to light the parlors in innumerable homes, and grease the wheels of multitudes of factories and shops. Yet in his home, the mighty magnate lived like a rather ordinary Midwestern business man. He had married a Cleveland girl in 1864, and the years brought him a son and three daughters. His life outside the office centered around them, and around the Baptist church. Through this he was led into a steadily widening program of gift-giving, which eventually became the major activity of his old age and set new patterns in charity.

The Rockefellers lived in a four-story brownstone house on West 54th

Rockefeller's brownstone in New York had a yard (left) where he often skated; it is now the garden of the Museum of Modern Art.

Street, which was big enough to be called a mansion. He had a skating rink built in the back yard, and could be seen on winter mornings, skimming along in a silk hat for a little exercise before going to the office. There were often guests at dinner, but Rockefeller kept no French chef (unlike most other millionaires), ate sparingly from the simple menus, and sometimes ordered only bread and milk for himself, topped off with an apple, which he ate just before bedtime.

He was a fond but firm father. All his children were educated at private schools, kept on short allowances, set to doing chores, and encouraged both in saving and in making regular charitable contributions from their earnings. His son, John D. Rockefeller, Jr., spent two winters doing hard manual work on the family country place near Cleveland. None of the children ever recalled hearing their parents' voices raised in complaint or anger. Their memories were of a house often full of guests—business associates, church workers, and their own youthful friends—with a good deal of amiable conversation, music, reading aloud, and laughter. Certainly there were no gloomy shadows cast by Rockefeller's enormous business cares.

As he grew older, the magnate broadened his scale of living. At the end of the century, he bought an estate near Tarrytown, New York, named Pocantico, and spent lavishly to landscape it according to his taste. He took great pleasure in this, as well as in the game of golf, which he learned in 1899 at the age of sixty. He was an enthusiastic player, and his frequent appearances on the course that he installed on the estate at Pocantico made him the target of cartoon humor. But despite his adoption of such rich men's pastimes, Rockefeller remained a curious paradox. In business and philanthropy his scale of thought was imperial and global. At home it could well be called comfortably suburban.

He continued his program of giving at least a tenth of his income, now colossal, to help others. Rockefeller was the first industrial prince to attempt to organize his charities. At first he made random donations to libraries, hospitals, asylums, and schools. These were sizable enough.

Rockefeller took up golf at sixty and still played regularly when he was ninety-four.

In 1892 alone, they added up to $1,350,000. Like some of his fellow millionaires (Vanderbilt, Duke, and Leland Stanford), he endowed a university. His initial gift of $600,000 in 1889, later increased many times over, enabled the University of Chicago to open its doors in 1892. It quickly became one of the nation's great intellectual centers—even though students jokingly recited a doxology of their own, "Praise John from whom oil blessings flow!"

By 1891 Rockefeller had hired an assistant, Frederick T. Gates, whose entire job was to supervise his philanthropies. Later, his son, John D.

Rockefeller, Jr., joined in this work. The plan they conceived was to create special institutions with a large original gift. The annual interest on this endowment would support continued good works in some chosen field. In 1901 the Rockefeller Institute for Medical Research was created to finance numerous advances and improvements in the teaching of medicine in the United States. The next year came the General Education Board, which finally spent itself out of business in 1965—after sixty years of generous assistance devoted to improving education, first in the South, and later in colleges and medical schools across the United States. And in 1913 the Rockefeller Foundation was set up. It carried on a huge program of disease control all over the world. Doctors fighting hookworm in the American South, yellow fever in Cuba, and sleeping sickness in Africa, were backed by funds which came from the Rockefeller fortune. Rockefeller had not only kept (in his own view) his promise to share his wealth with the Lord, but had managed to bring to charity the same massive organization that led him to his triumphs in the oil fields.

John D. Rockefeller, Sr. lived for two years short of a century, dying in 1937. He had seen Standard Oil dissolved into a number of separate, but well coordinated, companies after a government suit brought under the Sherman Antitrust Act, in 1911. (That 1890 legislation, intended to restore competition in industry, was chiefly inspired by the popular reaction to Standard's practices.) Rockefeller also lived to see petroleum products used in the internal combustion engine. Men could travel on wings and wheels because of the discovery and use of petroleum, which he had done so much to promote.

Rockefeller's fortune has been estimated at anywhere between two hundred and nine hundred million dollars. In making it, he had changed the idea that American business was a game in which many players had the opportunity to succeed. By eliminating the small businessman from oil refining, he ran counter to the spirit that made America a land of equality. But he had realized that in the complex modern world, the production of fuel for light and energy must take place on a highly organized basis. His vision foresaw the link between riggers drilling a well in Texas (or in Arabia or Venezuela) and customers buying naphtha in New York or Boston. Without master planning, the production and refining of oil would have remained uncoordinated, and the enormous industrial expansion, in which oil was vital, would never have been possible. Rockefeller provided that planning, at the cost of wiping out a part of America's economic individualism. Men still debate whether this made him a "robber baron" or an "industrial statesman." Whichever he was, he left a permanent mark on the twentieth century.

85

ADMINISTERING THE AVALANCHE

"Your fortune is rolling up like an avalanche! You must distribute it faster than it grows! If you do not, it will crush you." How seriously John D. Rockefeller and his son, John D., Jr. (right), took this admonition from a trusted advisor is shown by the extraordinary range of their philanthropies, estimated at well over $2,500,000,000. Their liberal gifts made possible the examination of a sick child at a Rockefeller-sponsored health clinic in India (bottom left), the creation of a Stravinsky ballet in New York (top left), and the acquisition of 30,000 acres in Wyoming by the Grand Teton National Park (center). The $8,500,000 site for the United Nations buildings (right), covering six Manhattan city blocks, was donated by John D. Rockefeller, Jr.

5

THE MONEY MOGUL

By 1910 the owners of America's industries were mighty men. Their decisions meant good or bad times for whole cities, states, and regions. Jobs and prosperity for thousands rode on a nod or a shake of their heads—or at least so most people believed. But in New York City, a passerby who looked in at a ground-floor window at No. 23 Wall Street might just catch a glimpse of a man who could make railroad presidents and million-dollar manufacturers tremble when he frowned. From a neat, almost bare desk, John Pierpont Morgan ruled a vast banking empire. Modern business could neither live nor grow without the backing of credit. The country believed, with good reason, that J. P. Morgan could grant or deny credit to the most mammoth corporations of the day and ranked him first among the titans of business.

Morgan looked the part of an emperor. He was tall, stiff-moustached,

Edward Steichen photographed the awesome J. P. Morgan in 1903. What seems to be a knife in his left hand is really a chair arm.

severe in appearance, with a fiery red nose inflamed by an incurable skin disease. His eyes were so fierce and dominating that nobody would dare snicker at that nose. J. P. Morgan made two United States Presidents meet his terms to save the country from financial panic. His great power and princely style of life made him a living symbol of the might of money. Men needed and feared him because early twentieth century business activities had become immensely complicated as a result of the work of such industrialists as Vanderbilt, Hill, and Rockefeller.

Morgan did not rise from rags to riches as did most of the other early captains of industry. He was born in Hartford, Connecticut, in April, 1837, to Junius Morgan, a successful merchant and broker who later became a prominent international banker. Young "J.P." was educated in Boston and Switzerland and spent two years at the University of Göttingen in Germany. He went into the banking business at the age of twenty-four, and by the time he was twenty-six had a personal annual income of more than fifty thousand dollars. This represented his profit from investment banking, a highly specialized business.

Commercial and savings banks accept deposits and make loans to individuals and small business houses. Investment banks do the same thing on a much larger scale and might be called bankers' banks. When a very large corporation needs to raise money, it can do so in several ways. One is to sell shares of stock, which represent ownership of its properties. Buying stock entitles stockholders to vote for a company's directors, and to receive a part of its profit (after business expenses are met) in the form of dividends. A corporation may also sell bonds. (Governments, too, sometimes float loans by the sale of bonds.) The bonds represent the corporation's promises to pay the bondholders a certain sum at the end of a fixed period, plus interest at regular intervals. Such payments are legal debts, and if they are not met the company can be declared bankrupt and forced out of business. Bondholders, however, are simply creditors of a corporation; they do not vote for its officers.

When corporations or governments sell stocks and bonds (or securities) amounting to millions, they cannot depend entirely on sales in small parcels if they are in any hurry to raise the money. They rely on great investment firms to find customers—usually other banks—who can make purchases in lots amounting to hundreds of thousands, and even millions of dol-lars. The banking house making the sale charges a commission for its services, and also earns interest and dividends on the securities which it buys for itself.

The power of a great investment bank, however, is far mightier than its profits. It directs a mighty flow of saved dollars to one industry or another. If it guides investment wisely, there is prosperity. But if it markets the securities of badly managed or unsound corporations, the savings of millions of people are wiped out when those companies fail. Banks themselves are forced into ruin, commerce is halted, factory wheels stop turning, and depression ravages the country.

This was the business, and those were the risks, of the young J. P. Morgan. He was thoroughly successful at it. His firm sold bonds for the Federal and state governments, and for private industry. Through partnerships with banks in London and Paris, he found European customers for American securities. Thus Morgan helped direct the flow of millions of dollars from Europe into the development of American industries, which could not grow without them. As the years went by, Morgan found himself concerned with protecting the investments he had encouraged others to make. This brought him into the field of industrial peacemaking.

In 1879 Morgan arranged for the private sale of a big block of stock in the New York Central Railroad, then being run by William H. Vander-

In the 1850's the New York Stock Exchange met somewhat informally in a crowded room on Wall Street. Brokers traded stocks by shouting buy and sell orders to clerks on the platform.

bilt, son of the old Commodore. Six years later, Morgan heard something that disturbed him. A bankrupt little railroad called the West Shore ran up the west side of the Hudson, parallel to the Central's east bank tracks to Albany. Morgan learned that the Pennsylvania Railroad was buying West Shore's depreciated bonds and was planning to build westward, to compete with the Central for the Great Lakes rail traffic. William Vanderbilt already knew of this and organized a company to build a line, from Philadelphia to Pittsburgh, to battle the "Pennsy" for the rich coal and iron business of the West. Engineers were even then grading the route.

To Morgan, the prospects were alarming. The two giant companies would conduct savage rate-cutting wars, and surely lose money. The price of both railroads' securities in the market would drop. The men to whom Morgan had sold Central stock would suffer, and financial freebooters might gain control of both companies. Something had to be done.

First Morgan arranged to return from a European trip on the same boat with William H. Vanderbilt, and had a long talk with him. Then, one warm July day, he took George B. Roberts, president of the Pennsylvania, for a cooling cruise up the East River on his private yacht. Whatever Morgan said must have been persuasive. The Pennsylvania dropped its plans to buy the West Shore, and the Central let the proposed new road across the southern part of its rival's

territory remain unbuilt. (Years later, in the 1930's, the roadbed was bought by the state, and the modern Pennsylvania Turnpike follows it for miles.)

So successful was this first effort at reducing competition that Morgan went on to others. In 1886 he got a number of railroad lines that owned coal mines to agree to fix coal prices and limit production, ending one source of big losses. And in 1889,

Scenes of frenzied selling erupted on the floor of the Stock Exchange (newly enlarged) during the depression of 1893. Stock prices tumbled by millions before Morgan intervened.

there was a meeting of the great and mighty of the railroad world in the library of Morgan's New York mansion. The presidents of almost every railroad east of Chicago—the Pennsylvania, the Erie, the Central, the Baltimore & Ohio, the Lehigh Valley, and the Lackawanna—were there. So were the heads of four or five of the country's biggest banking houses. Morgan proposed that the railroad rulers agree not to build needless competing lines in each other's territories; and in turn, the bankers promise not to finance any such raids. An agreement of this sort was finally reached, although it was not altogether kept. But J. P. Morgan was emerging as a man who disliked cutthroat competition, because it stifled business growth and reduced profits.

Four years later his real opportunity came. In 1893 the nation tumbled into an economic depression. Business stagnated; unemployed roamed the streets; and more than a hundred railroad companies, unable to pay their debts, were declared bankrupt. A sharp eye could have seen it coming.

In the 1870's and 1880's dozens of promoters had built railroads senselessly and hastily. Sometimes they built in the neighborhood of an existing line, hoping to blackmail it into buying them out. Sometimes they built to get land subsidies and loans from railroad-hungry communities. Sometimes they built merely to sell stock on the market at a quick profit. In all such cases, securities were is

sued far beyond any reasonable chance of dividends or repayments. Now the creditors were asking for their money.

Into this chaos stepped Morgan. He began to reorganize one road after another. Smaller lines were consolidated into bigger ones. Old bonds were replaced with new ones, due at a later date and paying less interest. New stock was issued to bring in fresh money but one thing was made clear: holders of this stock had to surrender their voting power and allow new boards of directors, many named by Morgan, to take over. Those directors specialized in saying "No." No rate wars. No competitive building. No new expenditures, unless absolutely necessary. No activities to interrupt the punctual payment of interest on those bonds behind which J. P. Morgan and Company had put its reputation for shrewdness. By 1899 Morgan-approved agents were laying down rules for the Erie, the Reading, and a group of railroads in the South.

Morgan's firm, of course, made vast profits from selling the new stocks and bonds of the reorganized lines. From his point of view, it was a small reward for creating a healthy, national transportation system. The railroads were certainly on a sounder financial footing. Investors were better off. And since everyone who puts money in a bank—or is paid by someone with money in a bank—has a stake in the country's financial health, the public presumably gained too.

There were, however, two sides to

the story. The people lost the benefit of improvements and lower rates that competition among the lines encouraged. Reorganized railroads were free to raise the price not only of passenger tickets, but of the rates for carrying fuel and foodstuffs. And Morgan's management did not frown on economies such as cutting services to out-of-the-way places, and reducing the wages of railroad employees. The country got railroad stability, order, and growth—but at a price.

As early as 1895 Morgan was a power in the land, but the next ten years were to show his even greater strength. The industrial machine constructed in the years that followed the Civil War needed tightening, tuning, and replacement of weak parts before it could go into high gear. That meant unity of action among its owners. The age of bigness was at hand. And Morgan showed just how big he was by coming to the rescue of the United States itself.

In the desperate depression years, gold alone claimed a value that was certain and steady. So many men exchanged their paper wealth for gold that there was a shortage in the supply of the precious metal—the basis of currency in numerous countries. The shortage at first was irritating. Speedily it became disturbing, even terrifying. The Government of the United States, which by law had to pay some of its obligations in gold, suddenly found late in 1894 that its own reserves—the stacks of gold that

J. PIERPONT MORGAN, UN
This Stirring American, Havin

94

EXANDER THE GREAT, HAS MORE WORLDS TO CONQUER.
ol of Our Railroads and Steel Business, is Reaching for the Shipping of the Universe.

After "re-Morganizing" the nation's railroads and steel industry, the master of the money trust announced his plan for a huge British-American shipping combine, a move that prompted this hostile cartoon of 1902.

it kept on hand to "back up" the currency—were dwindling fast. (The Treasury, like a bank, does not need to have enough cash on hand to pay off all its creditors at once, but it must always have a certain percentage of such a sum on hand.)

The reason for the decline in Federal gold reserves was that gold was being hoarded, and many firms and agencies that owed taxes were taking advantage of a legal right to pay the Government in other ways. In addition, because of the business slump caused by the depression, the amount of any kind of tax, customs, or other revenue was shrinking. The gold shortage was a real crisis. It brought the sudden, frightening prospect of a day when the Federal Government could no longer honor its promises to pay. Chief among these were the notes printed by the Treasury—the money in everyone's pocket. If the day were to come when a dollar bill would not buy anything, when a merchant would demand gold or jewels or goods for a sack of flour or a yard of cloth, then the entire economy might collapse.

Many men at the time argued that silver, which was plentiful, was as good a basis for currency as gold. William Jennings Bryan ran for President in 1896—and lost—on just that platform. Others believed that as long as people had faith in the Government's ability to collect and spend taxes, its money would be honored.

President Grover Cleveland and his Secretary of the Treasury did not

Able, agreeable Charles M. Schwab, who had helped create United States Steel, became that gigantic corporation's president.

share this optimism. In their view gold was desperately needed. Early in 1895 they got in touch with J. P. Morgan and another banker, August Belmont. Morgan told them he and Belmont could help line up a syndicate of American and European bankers who would get together sixty-two million dollars in gold and sell it to the United States in return for a series of Government bonds. Of course, there would be a commission in it for the bankers, plus the interest on the bonds. When the deal was completed, there were outraged howls that the Government had needlessly enriched private bankers instead of appealing to the people through a public bond sale. But Morgan was deaf to them. He felt that he had saved the nation's credit in a desperate hour. So, in fact, did President Cleveland.

A man big enough to be the Government's banker in a time of need was also able to undertake the largest transaction in business history, and in 1901 Morgan did just that.

The industry involved was basic to the life of the new century. steel. By 1900 steel production was divided among a number of great concerns specializing in the making of steel ingots, wire, nails, sheets, girders, hoops, and other products. Several big steel manufacturers approached Morgan to ask his help in creating a supercombination that would put together iron mines, ore-carrying vessels, blast furnaces, and plants that made steel articles. Such a giant, efficiently controlling steel production from the mining of ore in Minnesota to the sale of nails in a hardware store, would make the industry enormously productive—and profitable. Morgan liked what he heard. The first essential was to get the Carnegie Steel Company, the biggest and best manufacturer of crude steel, into the organization. This meant buying out Andrew Carnegie, the genial but tough steelmaster whose story is told in the next chapter. Carnegie, as it happened, was ready to retire from business life, but at his own price. He and Morgan did not meet directly, preferring to negotiate through Charles M. Schwab, Carnegie's chief executive and right-

hand man. The price Carnegie wanted for his plants and equipment was approximately $493,000,000. Schwab met Morgan in New York and handed him a sheet of paper with this figure pencilled on it by Carnegie; Morgan glanced at it, and said: "I accept." Later on, Morgan called on Carnegie to arrange the details of this astounding transaction, and as the banker left, he said, "Mr. Carnegie, I want to congratulate you on being the richest man in the world." A year or so later, Carnegie and Morgan met once again, by chance. Carnegie said that he had made one mistake in selling out. "I should have asked you a hundred million more than I did," he told Morgan. "Well," was the answer, "you would have got it if you had."

In March, 1901, the newspapers finally announced the creation of the United States Steel Corporation. It merged nine existing large concerns and put under one management sixty per cent of the country's entire steel making industry. Its stock, which was to be sold by a syndicate headed by J. P. Morgan and Co., had a face value of one billion, four hundred million dollars. Morgan had brought into being the first billion-dollar corporation. (The United States Government itself had only begun spending one billion dollars a year in 1890.)

The country was frightened by such immensity, yet it admired the vision of the promoters. Morgan's activities between 1901 and 1903 did nothing to quiet these fears. As mentioned in

Chapter 3, he helped James J. Hill and E. H. Harriman acquire a railroad monopoly of the entire Northwest through the Northern Securities Company. In 1902 J. P. Morgan's firm arranged the merger of six trans-Atlantic shipping lines into an ocean-going holding company, the International Mercantile Marine. (Its best-known ship, unfortunately, was the ill-fated *Titanic*, which sank in 1912, with a loss of more than a thousand lives, after striking an iceberg.) In the same year Morgan took an active part in creating the International Harvester Company, which merged Cyrus Mc-Cormick's firm with its biggest rivals, and thus controlled eighty per cent of the harvester business.

These were only a few of many Morgan-financed mergers, and it began to look to many people as if Morgan money backed—and Morgan's friends and partners directed—every supertrust that was organized. Was Morgan becoming the czar of American industry? The President of Yale warned that unless trusts were curbed, there might some day be an emperor in Washington. And there was a joke about the newspaper editor who, when Morgan was quoted as saying "America is good enough for me," quipped, "Whenever he doesn't like it, he can give it back to us."

Morgan's last big demonstration of power came during the financial panic of 1907, when a sudden plunge in stock prices, followed by the collapse of a bank, threw investors into a spasm of fear that another big depression was at hand. By rushing to withdraw savings and sell securities, they threatened to drive other banks into bankruptcy and bring on the very crash they dreaded. Morgan was attending a convention of the Episcopal Church in Richmond, Virginia. He took an express train back to his office and began a round-the-clock series of conferences with other bankers and stockbrokers.

In the course of ninety-six hours, he arranged to lend $25,000,000 of his own bank's funds to other banks, bought a New York City bond issue for $30,000,000, and got other, still solvent banks and trust companies to put up a $25,000,000 fund for paying depositors and buying stocks to sustain prices. The idea was that if the public saw the country's biggest banks *buying* securities, they would regain confidence and stop panic sales. Of course, if they failed to do so, then Morgan and his associates would go down with the rest. But the gamble paid off: the market leveled, wavered, and then started to climb, not, however, before a dramatic episode had taken place.

At the height of the crisis, a large brokerage house, Moore and Schley, was nearly at the end of its rope. The firm's biggest assets consisted of most

The stately portico of Morgan's office at the corner of Wall and Broad streets was a few steps from the Stock Exchange (center).

98

*Thousands of worried investors, "gathered as if to watch a fire,"
jammed Wall Street during the dark days of October, 1907. Early on
the twenty-ninth, Morgan initialed the promise, written on his library
notepaper (right), to bolster New York's credit with a $30,000,000 loan.*

of the stock of the Tennessee Coal and Iron Company, an independent concern. Moore and Schley now proposed that they sell this company directly to the United States Steel Corporation. This move would get them out of their financial troubles, boost the price of United States Steel stock, help break the slump in the market, and, incidentally, eliminate yet another competitor of the steel trust.

President Theodore Roosevelt had already made a reputation as a "trust-buster." In 1904 his Attorney General had prosecuted the Northern Securities Company under the Sherman Antitrust Act. Morgan and the officers of United States Steel took no chances with the President. They insisted on an understanding from Washington that the take over of Tennessee Coal and Iron would not bring United States Steel into court. Roosevelt was persuaded by his financial advisers that his approval was needed, and in an indirect way he gave it. Once again, Morgan had saved the country's finances. And once again, he had done so at a good profit, since United States Steel shares rose as a result of the new merger. More interesting, J. P. Morgan had again dealt with an American President as an equal, not as a private citizen with the head of the Federal Government.

When Morgan died in 1913, at the age of seventy-five, a new President, Woodrow Wilson, had taken office. He had been elected on a platform that included promises to curb the great power of the financiers who held directorships in the nation's leading companies—the members of what people called the Money Trust. In time, this power would be somewhat restricted. But basically, the pattern had already been set.

The great investment houses would remain at the center of the economy, because old-fashioned unrestricted competition was dead. It was inevitable that mighty industries, with world-wide markets and multimillion dollar plants, would be consolidated into ever larger units. And it was equally inevitable that this process would require enormous quantities of money, gathered and controlled by banks. Capital, whether in private hands or government hands, rules the modern age. In this sense J. P. Morgan's career pointed forward, and he clearly belongs with today's industrialized world.

Morgan was not the country's

AMERICA AGAINST THE TRUSTS

In the late 1880's, when the Federal Government seemed unable or unwilling to take action against the abuses of the trusts, public outcry reached a high pitch. Americans saw bitter truth in Thomas Nast's "Home of the Trusts" (left) and Joseph Keppler's "Bosses of the Senate" (above); and from all directions came outraged protest against the control that was exercised by the few over the lives of the many. Such savage criticism finally goaded the Government into action. In December of 1889, a few months after these two cartoons appeared, Ohio's Senator John Sherman—General William Tecumseh Sherman's brother—(right) introduced a bill to outlaw the trusts. Congress passed the Sherman Antitrust Act in 1890, but for more than a decade it was ignored. The law came alive in 1904, when Theodore Roosevelt used it to break up the Northern Securities Company, brainchild of Morgan and railroaders Hill and Harriman. When Roosevelt left the White House in 1909 and went on an African safari, a still-angry Morgan remarked, "I hope the first lion he meets does his duty."

wealthiest man. His estate, when he died, was estimated at sixty-eight millions—small by comparison with that of Rockefeller, for example, whose donations alone added up to half a billion. But Morgan spent lavishly, and he had champagne tastes. His fortune, which contrasted so sharply with the poverty of millions, was untouched by the heavy taxes of the present day. (The Federal income tax only went into effect in the year of his death.) Although he gave liberally, especially to the Episcopal Church of which he was a devout member, much of his money went into his style of living.

Like other millionaires, he had a number of residences. There was a mansion on New York's Madison Avenue, and another on the west shore of the Hudson; an Adirondack summer camp, and a summer cottage at fashionable Newport, Rhode Island. Since he spent three months of every year in Europe as he grew older, there was a town house in London and an English country estate named Dover House. And suites were always ready for him at hotels in London, Paris, and Rome. What marked these homes and set them apart from others was the magnificent works of art with which Morgan filled them. He bought paintings by the old masters, as well as statues, jewelry, armor, furniture, and precious old books and manuscripts. Eventually, he built a complete library, now standing at 36th Street and Madison Avenue, in New

York City, to house the rare books that were the pride of his collections. Toward the end of his life Morgan lent the Metropolitan Museum some of his most valuable paintings, and after his death his son gave many of them to the Museum's permanent collection. They are housed in the Pierpont Morgan wing, in honor of his father. Morgan's collections, at the time of his death, were valued at about fifty million dollars.

When Morgan traveled on rails, it was by private car, of course. And on the water he had a succession of private yachts. The last, the *Corsair III*, was 302 feet long and could cross the Atlantic. The cost of its fuel and crew was beyond computation. Someone once asked Morgan how much it cost to keep a yacht. He is supposed to have replied, "If you have to ask, you can't afford it."

His personal mannerisms were those of an autocrat. He was hard to approach, and had few close friends. Although he could be very generous (he would, now and then, take parties of friends to jewelry or fur shops, and invite them to help themselves at his expense), people dreaded offending him. They felt uncomfortable in his presence. Above all, many were afraid of making some unfortunate remark about his red nose. There is a story that Mrs. Dwight Morrow, the wife of another banker, once invited Morgan to tea, promising to introduce him to her two little daughters, one of whom, Anne Morrow, later became a poet and the wife of the famous aviator, Charles Lindbergh. Mrs. Morrow was in mortal fear that the children would make some tactless remark, as children will, about Morgan's remarkable nose. They were carefully coached not to stare at him, or to comment upon the great man's appearance. Finally the day of his visit came. The girls were brought into the parlor, and a few moments of conversation followed. The hostess was on pins and needles until her daughters left. When they had gone Mrs. Morrow, sighing with inward relief, turned and asked: "Do you, Mr. Morgan, take one or two lumps of sugar in your nose?"

One does not laugh, after all, at royalty. And J. P. Morgan was royal in his way. He entertained blue-bloods in his art galleries and on his yacht with no sense of social inferiority. The Kaiser lunched on the *Corsair*, and the Queen of England admired Morgan's paintings. The Queen Mother of Italy, the Chief Secretary to the Pope, and countless dukes and duchesses received him in their homes.

The First World War destroyed most of the glitter of this European aristocracy. The social changes that followed tended to make American millionaires, too, less frivolous in their personal spending, and more apt to take pride in their foundations or their public services. (It is worth noting that Nelson Rockefeller, a grandson of John D., succeeded W. Averell Harriman, the son of Edward H. Harriman, as governor of New York. Both men prefer to be known for their careers in government, though the founders of the family fortunes were contemptuous of "mere politicians.") The truly rich of today are concerned with human relations and with a favorable public image.

Morgan's public image was that of an uncrowned monarch. He chose to have it so. Men could say of him when he died, as Prince Hamlet said of his father: "[We] shall not look upon his like again."

Morgan brandishes his cane at a photographer. In the street "he did not dodge, or walk in and out . . . He simply barged along . . . the embodiment of power and purpose."

6
THE HAPPIEST MILLIONAIRE

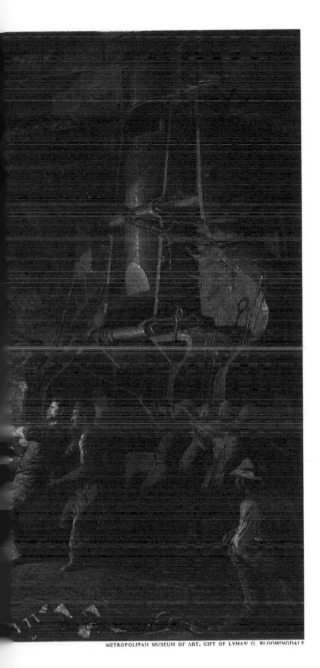

One March day in 1901 Andrew Carnegie signed the papers that sold his steelmaking properties to the United States Steel Corporation. His personal share of the purchase price, invested in five per cent bonds, guaranteed him an income of more than $1,000,000 a month for the rest of his life. His thoughts may well have turned back fifty-two years to the day he got his first job. He was thirteen years old and the job was changing bobbins (spools of thread) in a cotton mill, from sunrise to sunset each day except Sunday, for $1.20 a week. He had come a long way in half a century.

It was no wonder, then, that Carnegie was an optimist. "All my ducks are swans," he once said, and declared his motto to be "the truth of evolution," which was "All is well since all grows better." He rose to wealth on a great tide of national development, scientific discovery, and expansion in manufacturing. He saw his career as clear proof that a kindly universe took special care of him, and of the English-speaking countries on both sides of the Atlantic between which he divided his affection. For eighteen years after his retirement, he devoted his life to a program of gift-giving that he believed would help to make the world an even better place. These donations

Sweating ironworkers strain to weld a cannon barrel at the West Point Foundry in 1877. Canny investment in the growing iron and steel business made Carnegie's fortune.

added up to nearly $350,000,000. Along with them went thousands of words written by Carnegie about his favorite subject—himself. Of all the great business tycoons, he was the one who best combined good luck, good management, and foresight with charm and conceit. The story of his two careers—as a maker and a giver of wealth—shows all of these forces at work.

The Carnegie story did not begin happily. Ironically, the same machine age that made Andrew's fortune threw his father out of work in Scotland in the 1840's. William Carnegie was a handloom weaver in the historic town of Dunfermline. Though he and his wife became desperately poor in terms of money, their legacy to Andrew and his younger brother Tom was rich in every other way. William was an insatiable reader, with a romantic devotion to Scottish history. A political radical himself, William married the daughter of a prominent agitator in the cause of political reform. Margaret Carnegie was the dominant influence in the household, and it was she who had the idea of emigrating to America, where the entire family could make a new start. They borrowed passage money from a friend, sold their household possessions, and, in

In this 1849 view of Pittsburgh, a year after the Carnegies' arrival, its rivers are full of boats, and factory smoke darkens the sky. Below, Andrew (left) and his brother Thomas pose in their 1851 Sunday best.

1848, made the seven-weeks-long voyage from Glasgow to New York.

The Carnegie family settled near Pittsburgh, and William found work in a cotton factory. Young Andrew's first job, in the same mill, was taken to help in the family's struggle to make ends meet. Soon after, he went to work in another factory, for sixty cents more a week, tending a boiler in the basement, a dark, cheerless job. But almost at once his luck turned.

The factory owner, finding out that young Carnegie had some schooling and wrote neatly, promoted him to office duties. Andrew was grateful to move to a job that was cleaner, lighter,

109

Thousands of nineteenth-century children like Carnegie toiled from dawn to dusk at the jobs of changing bobbins in a textile mill (left), separating unusable slate from coal (above), or making paper flowers in a tenement (below).

and less exhausting. He was also able to save some of his energies for constant sparetime reading. A retentive memory and alert probing mind enabled him to develop his interests in politics and science, as well as in the classics of English and Scottish literature. His ability to quote Burns and Shakespeare freely would stand him in good stead later, when he mixed with men of better formal education than he. He was learning to use to the full every opportunity and advantage that came his way.

Presently a friend of the Carnegies' offered Andrew a job as a telegraph messenger, at $2.50 a week. Gratefully, he took the upward step and gave the work attentive study. As he said in later life, whatever he undertook he must "push inordinately." Soon he knew many of Pittsburgh's leading businessmen by sight and could deliver messages to them instantly. More important, while waiting in the telegraph office for messages to come in, he taught himself the Morse code and was able to graduate to the rank of operator. His speed and intelligence were soon noticed by Thomas A. Scott, then Pittsburgh-division superintendent of the Pennsylvania Railroad, who hired him as personal clerk and telegraph operator.

Thus, at seventeen, Andrew Carnegie had reason to feel that hard work and a pleasing way with important men were the first steps to success. His new salary of $35 per month seemed enormous; he hardly knew what to do with the money. When his father died two years later, Carnegie welcomed the opportunity to become his mother's main support, and took the responsibility seriously enough to remain unmarried until after her death in 1886. He was still reading widely, visiting the theater now and then, and writing occasional letters to Pittsburgh newspapers, or even to the far-off New York *Tribune*.

Carnegie's literary ambitions did not interfere with his learning railroading from the bottom up. One morning that study paid off. An accident had temporarily tied up a section of the Pennsylvania's line. Trains could not move until dispatching orders were sent out and wrecking crews assigned. And Superintendent Scott could not be located. Andrew Carnegie thought for a while, and then began tapping his key swiftly. He sent out a series of telegrams, under Scott's name, that cleared the track, untangled the snarl, and put traffic on the road once more. When Scott finally appeared, Carnegie rather nervously told him what he had done. Scott said not a word but later boasted to others about the exploit of his "little white-haired devil."

Scott's appreciation was shown in a quick series of promotions for Carnegie. By the time the Civil War broke out, in 1861, Andrew had Scott's old job as superintendent of the Pittsburgh division. When Scott was called to Washington to take charge of railroads and telegraphs, as an Assistant

Secretary of War, it was Carnegie, aged twenty-five, whom he took to work with him.

In fact, Scott had shown another interest in Carnegie's career that was to prove even more significant. Scott was a master businessman, who would later become president of the Pennsylvania Railroad as well as of the Union Pacific and the Texas & Pacific railroads, and he knew a shrewd investment when he saw one. When he suggested, in 1855, that if Carnegie had $500 he would be wise to buy ten shares of stock in the Adams Express Company, Andrew did not hesitate to mortgage the home he had bought for his mother to make the investment. His first dividend came soon after. From this beginning grew a regular series of investments. First small sums, and then larger ones, went into:

a bank, an oil well or two, a railroad, a company for manufacturing sleeping cars, and an insurance company. As fast as dividends were earned— they came generously in the economic boom of Civil War days—they were plowed into new stock. Carnegie was a Pittsburgh man, and since Pittsburgh was a center of the iron trade, he naturally began betting on the future of iron.

In 1865 Carnegie joined with H. J. Linville, John L. Piper, and Aaron Shiffler, who designed bridges for the Pennsylvania Railroad, to form the Keystone Bridge Company. Its purpose was to build the iron bridges that were rapidly replacing wooden ones on progressive railroads. In 1864 he organized a railmaking concern, and in 1866 a locomotive works. In 1867 Andrew, his brother Tom, and fellow

Carnegie's Keystone Bridge Company undertook to span the Mississippi in 1867. St. Louis's famous Eads Bridge (above) was opened in 1874; it had cost $10,000,000. Andrew Carnegie himself sold $4,000,000 worth of its bonds to banker Junius Morgan.

Like a Horatio Alger hero, Andrew Carnegie, born in a Scottish weaver's cottage (above), returned to his home the richest man in the world. There he bought Skibo Castle (right) and flew the Union Jack and the Stars and Stripes from his flagpole.

Pittsburghers Thomas Miller, Henry Phipps, and Andrew Kloman as partners, set up the Union Iron Mills.

Looking after these investments was a full-time job, and in 1865 Carnegie left the Pennsylvania Railroad's payroll. But he kept his friendship with Tom Scott, and with the Pennsylvania's president, J. Edgar Thomson, which helped him to get plenty of orders for his ironware from their railroad. In turn, recognizing Carnegie as a supersalesman, the Pennsylvania sent him to Europe, in 1872, to sell five million dollars' worth of its bonds. The job earned him a commission of $150,000.

Carnegie's major contribution to the various firms in which he was a partner was his knack of winning in-fluential friends. The factories were superintended by men like Andrew Kloman, a skilled foundry foreman, while others, like Henry Phipps, deftly managed bookkeeping transactions. Carnegie moved his headquarters, in 1867, from Pittsburgh to New York, a better center for sales operations. To John W. Garrett, Baltimore & Ohio Railroad president, he sold many an iron-bridge contract, in part because the two men shared a fondness for Scottish poet Robert Burns. In 1869 he sold four million dollars' worth of bonds to Junius Morgan (J. P. Morgan's banker father) in London, after impressing the financier by using the then-new and expensive Atlantic cable to relay a question to America and get an immediate reply.

For fifty years Carnegie kept this memorandum among his most treasured papers. It outlines a life plan that was never fulfilled.

Carnegie seemed to take more pleasure in influencing men than in making money at this time. A private memorandum, written when he was thirty-three years old, reveals his feelings. He was earning $50,000 a year. He hoped, in two more years, to retire from business management on this income, settle near Oxford to "get a thorough education," and buy up a "newspaper or live review and give the general management of it attention, taking a part in public matters." Between 1869 and 1872, however, in the course of his frequent trips to England, Carnegie became convinced that an important new age of steel was just dawning. He determined to create a huge supply of that "gleam-ing metal upon which civilization advances." That meant transferring his investments into steel—or, as he later described it, his policy became "to put all good eggs in one basket and then watch that basket." He was to have thirty years of watching before he could retire.

In fact, Carnegie was jumping on a moving bandwagon. The first cheap method of manufacturing steel on a large scale had been patented by an English inventor, Sir Henry Bessemer, in 1855. The Bessemer process was simple and spectacular: air was forced, under pressure, into a huge, egg-shaped blast furnace full of molten pig iron; the impurities in the iron were oxidized, under intense heat, and shot away in a shower of sparks from the top of the converter. The liquid metal left behind needed only the addition of ferromanganese to become top-quality steel. English manufacturers were soon making their fortunes with this process. By 1870 American pioneers like Alexander Holley were beginning to turn out Bessemer steel on more than an experimental basis in the United States.

American railroads had an apparently inexhaustible appetite for tough, flexible, long-lasting steel rails. Armies and navies needed steel guns and steel plate; and bridges and buildings

"Steel is king!" cried Carnegie after seeing the Bessemer steelmaking process (right) in action. Its drama always thrilled him.

View of Dravo Works

Genuine Conne...me C

H.C.FRICK COKE COMPANY

Mining Coal

5000 OVENS, CAPACITY 8750 TON

Process of Manufacturing Coke at the Works o

H.C. FRICK COKE COMP

CONNELLSVILLE COKE REGION

POST OFFICE, PITTSBURGH PA.

Frick's coke empire at Connellsville, Pennsylvania, made him a profitable partner for Carnegie. Above, center, coal is dumped into a line
of beehive ovens that will bake it into coke. When workers with hoses
have cooled the coke down, others carry it in barrows to waiting trains.

116

View of Trotter Shaft.

Watering and Drawing Coke.

would shortly need steel girders and supports. There was a market for millions of tons of steel a year, and a tariff of $28 a ton on imported steel reserved that market for American manufacturers. Carnegie saw Pittsburgh as an ideal center for steelmaking activities. Surrounded by beds of coal that would make good coke (a vital ingredient in steelmaking), it had easy connections by rail and ship to the great iron ore beds of Lake Superior. In addition, the city was full of experienced metallurgists and engineers who had learned their business in the iron trade.

In 1873 Carnegie and his partners built a steel mill at Braddock, Pennsylvania, and named it after the president of the Pennsylvania Railroad, J. Edgar Thomson. It was a booming success from the start. Carnegie had a genius for surrounding himself with smart men. One of his master strokes was putting a sturdy Welsh Civil War veteran, "Captain" William Jones, in charge of the army of workmen. Bill Jones drove his sweaty legions of American, Welsh, and Irish "hands" to break one production record after another. Years later Carnegie told of trying to reward Jones with a partnership in the company and of being turned down.

"I don't want to have my thoughts running on business," Jones said. "I have enough trouble looking after these works. Just give me a hell of a salary if you think I'm worth it."

"All right, Captain, the salary of

the President of the United States is yours."

"That's the talk," said the little Welshman.

Carnegie tirelessly booked orders for his steel mill, exerting all his charm and ability to do so. Yet he was a hard man as well as a capable and genial one. He constantly needled his production teams for new achievements. (Once, he was explaining to his plant officials how much relief he got from business cares on his yearly vacations. "And, oh Lord," said Bill Jones, "think of the relief we all get.") Increased output meant lower costs, so Carnegie relentlessly undersold competitors, and refused to join in any of the price-fixing agreements that were becoming common in industry during the 1880's. He reduced steel rail prices from $160 a ton in 1875 to $17 a ton at the century's end, and he could still turn a neat profit.

The little Scot shrewdly invested in ore lands and ships to carry the precious minerals from mine to blast furnace. In 1882, to protect his supply of coke, he made an alliance with Henry Clay Frick, a sharp-dealing ex-store clerk who had bought the best coking coal lands in Pennsylvania. Seven years later, Frick became a Carnegie partner and chairman of the firm. He was noted for hiring Italian, Hungarian, and Slavic workers who were hard to unionize, and driving them mercilessly. Carnegie kept away from this end of the business as much as possible. But after the bloody Homestead strike of 1892, when Frick ordered out Pinkerton armed guards to control the strikers at Carnegie's Homestead steel mills, and a running battle ensued, public outcry was directed as much at Carnegie, who had been on vacation in Scotland, as at Frick himself. The two men later parted company as the result of a bitter quarrel.

As the steel business got bigger, Carnegie bought out rival plants and issued stock, but never to the public at large. He shared it with a few partners, but kept most of it himself. If one partner chose to sell out, the others took over his interest. Although Carnegie and his associates drove a hard bargain, the partnership was generally open to enterprising young men who rose from the ranks. One of them was Charles M. Schwab, who started as a dollar-a-day laborer and ended by replacing Frick as Carnegie's chief lieutenant.

By 1900 the United States had become the world's leader in steel production. Under Carnegie's continuing policy of keeping control tightly in his own hands, driving down costs, and outselling competitors, the Carnegie Steel Company was earning incredible profits. In 1900 they came to $40,000,000, of which Carnegie's own share was $25,000,000. The eggs in his basket had indeed done well.

The end of Carnegie's active career shows a side of his nature that he often kept hidden. He sometimes liked to give the impression that his success was due to his ability to hire men, in his words, "far cleverer than myself," and to back them when they ordered new and costly improvements in his plants. But Carnegie was no figurehead. In 1900 it became known that he was eager to sell out, and retire. The manufacture of finished steel articles was then largely in the hands of a few supercorporations: the Federal Steel Company, the National Tube Company, American Steel and Wire, American Tin Plate, and American Steel Hoop. The heads of these concerns decided that it would be profitable to have their own supply of crude steel, independent of Carnegie. They announced plans to erect blast furnaces and rolling mills. Their reasoning was that a tired Carnegie would easily be induced, by the threat of a price war, to sell out to a steelmaking combine on its own terms.

Into Carnegie's eyes came the light of battle. Telegraphed orders from Skibo Castle, his summer retreat in the Scottish highlands, bombarded Pittsburgh. The Carnegie Steel Company promptly declared it was going to manufacture its own forms of finished steel. It would open factories to produce tubes and steel rods. Perhaps later it would manufacture wire and tin plate too. Just for good measure, it would build a new railroad from Pittsburgh to the Atlantic and take away the steel traffic of the Pennsylvania and the Baltimore & Ohio.

Brutal violence erupted in July, 1892, when Frick's hired guards attempted to land from barges (above) and take over the Homestead works from a mob of strikers, ten thousand strong.

THE MACMILLION.

"How much have I given away?" Carnegie once asked his secretary. It was $324,657,399. "Wherever did I get all that money?" exclaimed the philanthropist whom a 1901 British cartoon (left) christened "The Macmillion" after his gift of $10,000,000 to four Scottish universities. At right, Carnegie and his wife pay a 1910 visit to the $22,000,000 Carnegie Institute he endowed in Pittsburgh.

The other steel giants did not want a war that would endanger their own investments, and neither did J. P. Morgan. He arranged to have Carnegie bought out for almost half a billion dollars. Even at sixty-five, Andrew Carnegie knew how to meet threats with threats. He had outlasted his enemies in a game of bluff.

Now, at last, Carnegie was free to travel, to study, to meet the great— and to give! The why and wherefore of his charities was spelled out in a number of articles and books. The most famous of the articles appeared in 1889, and became known by the title it was given when reprinted in England, "The Gospel of Wealth."

Carnegie said Darwin's theory of evolution proved that life was a struggle among species for existence. Only the fittest survived. Business life, too, was a war for survival. Those who came out on top of the competitive heap were naturally the fittest. The small businessman who could not compete with the large, efficient corporation might seem to suffer. Evolution was hard on the dinosaur, too. But the human race was better off in the long run with a flood of cheap, mass-produced goods as its compensation for loss of individualism.

It was a law of nature therefore, that some men became wealthy. They were gifted with a natural talent for

120

outstripping others in money-making, under the "law of competition." But they had a duty to perform. They must use their surplus wealth to promote the good of the community. They must not squander their money in piecemeal charity, but instead support those activities that helped the "fittest" of the next generation to emerge. "The man who dies rich, dies disgraced," Carnegie ended.

This was rather like John D. Rockefeller's idea of himself as a "steward" of God, but Carnegie, a free thinker, replaced God with evolution. His point was that much of the surplus wealth of a growing society was bound to flow into the hands of a particular small group of men, not just because they were lucky, or crafty, or simply smart and hard-working. It was because nature herself had stamped them as "the best." This handful of millionaires should then decide how the multiplied millions of new wealth should be used among their less favored fellow humans.

Conceited or not, Carnegie was a happy man. Few men have a fortune to give away in the promotion of their pet ideas. He did. His charities reflected all his favorite notions. As a boy he had loved to read, and he still believed that bookish boys were not likely to be idle or wasteful. So he gave $60,000,000 to build, or help build, some 2,800 library buildings in the United States and the United Kingdom. Another $30,000,000 went to various British and American universities. Because the marvels of science seemed to Carnegie the key to man's eternal advancement, he donated approximately $22,000,000 each to a Carnegie Institute in Washington and another in Pittsburgh, and $125,000,000 to the Carnegie Corporation of New York. All three fostered research not only in the natural and social sciences, but in the legal and educational fields as well.

Carnegie also thought that music should always bring joy to the worship of God, and he gave $6,000,000 to a special fund for buying church organs. Another $29,000,000 went to endow pensions for underpaid college professors. Pension funds for selected

steelworkers absorbed millions more. A specific fund was set up to provide recreation and education for the people of his native town of Dunfermline, and the Carnegie Hero Funds gave medals as well as pensions for acts of unusual bravery in peacetime.

Managing these many projects kept Carnegie from feeling old and used up. He was showered with honorary degrees by universities, given civic honors in innumerable towns, and introduced on equal terms to some of the most eminent men of the day. He was proud to claim friendship with Presidents Cleveland and Theodore Roosevelt; with Britain's Prime Ministers Gladstone and Lloyd George; and with writers like Mark Twain, Matthew Arnold, and John Morley.

Among Carnegie's favorite projects was the promotion of world peace. Though some of the steel he sold went into arms, Carnegie detested and abhorred war. He longed to see closer cooperation between the two English-speaking giants, the United States and Great Britain. He gave $1,500,000 to build the Peace Palace at The Hague; and $10,000,000 more, in 1910, to establish the Carnegie Endowment for International Peace, which was supposed to promote ways of abolishing war. Yet this last-named Carnegie charity had the saddest fate

of all. In August of 1914 the world he had believed so modern and progressive *did* go to war. In the notes he was making for his autobiography, Carnegie sadly wrote, "Men slaying each other like wild beasts! I dare not relinquish all hope." His patriotism forced him to approve first Britain's and then America's entry into the bitter fight which dragged on for four years and cost nearly ten million lives. Steel became associated almost exclusively with the material for shells, cannons, and bayonets; and Carnegie, for whom it had been the embodiment of progress, grieved profoundly. The happy, bustling old philanthropist suddenly retired from the public eye, and broke off his memoirs at the year 1914. In 1919, after a brief illness, he died. As his wife said, "His heart was broken."

The career of the happiest millionaire ended, after all, with a sense of defeat. Perhaps evolution did not always work in a kindly and improving fashion, as he had believed. Nevertheless, it *did* keep on working. The year Andrew Carnegie died was the heyday for a man whom some called "the last billionaire." He was Henry Ford, who put America in a wheeled contraption made of Carnegie steel and driven by Rockefeller's petroleum. With him, a new age of industry was to open—the era of mass production, of unionism, of automation— and the period when one man could wield absolute power in business was to close forever.

It was said of Carnegie that he had half a dozen personalities, by turns harsh, humorous, or benevolent, as in the portrait at left by H. R. Butler. Shrewdness won him customers; charm made many into friends.

CONSPICUOUS CONSUMPTION

By 1890 America, land of equal opportunity, was the home of the millionaire: one per cent of the people owned half of the nation's vast wealth. In 1899 economist Thorstein Veblen described the behavior of the rich as "conspicuous consumption of valuable goods as a means of reputability." Incredible sums were spent on indulging their desire for magnificence. John Jacob Astor's $20,000,000 fortune enabled his descendants to rule New York society. His grandson William, in 1878, commissioned the painting (above) of his family, aristocratically posed in their Fifth Avenue mansion. Commodore Vanderbilt's grandson George built a $5,000,000 replica of a French chateau (lower right) in North Carolina and christened it, suitably, "Biltmore." The "observation drawing room" (upper right) was the showpiece of the private train J. P. Morgan once rented at $500 a day for the trip from New York to San Francisco, after remodeling the baggage car to hold his vintage wines.

7

AMERICA ON WHEELS

In 1914 when the First World War broke out, most of the early captains of industry were dead or retired. The corporations that they had created were run by boards of directors, whose chairmen and members were rich and powerful but not entirely free to operate as they wished. They were subject to the wishes of the great banking houses that financed them. Increasingly, they needed lawyers to help them understand and apply (or avoid) a growing body of government regulations. After many years of public criticism of highhanded business tactics, industrial leaders were beginning to

To "build a motorcar for the great multitude" was the goal to which Henry Ford applied his genius, a concept that radically altered the life of every American and the face of

worry about how their actions would look to the press, and accordingly to seek advice from public relations experts. The multimillionaire who delighted in a price war, or in knocking out a rival and taking over a big territory, or in an inflated stock promotion, was being replaced by a quieter kind of operator.

The year 1914 also saw Henry Ford, automobile manufacturer of Detroit, make headlines in newspapers all over the United States with a breathtaking announcement. Henceforth, the minimum wage in his plants would be a previously unheard of five dollars per day. After that, Ford was rarely out of the public eye. A ruggedly independent, often bullheaded production genius, Ford was full of messages for the world. By the time his life ended in 1947, he was supposed to have made a billion dollars by putting America on wheels. He was scarred by battles with bankers, labor unions, newspapers, and courts. He had been denounced as a tyrant and a crank, and hailed as a prophet. Through it all he went his own stubborn way, telling his opponents and the entire nation exactly what he thought of them and still selling millions of cars. He was unique. He was Henry Ford. His story is a fitting end to a tale that began with another tempestuous lord of transportation, Cornelius Vanderbilt.

America itself. His dream soon became reality. Here, photographed in 1913, is one day's output of chassis for the Ford Model T. The basic price of the finished car was $550.

In 1903, when Ford posed for this picture, the Ford Motor Company sold its first car.

Ford was born on a farm near Dearborn, Michigan, in 1863, when the Civil War was killing men and making fortunes, and Rockefeller and Carnegie were investing in the new fields of oil and iron. Henry did not care for farm work. From the start, his passion was machinery, large and small. He was fascinated by the steam-driven threshing machines that traveled from farm to farm during the harvest season. He also enjoyed taking apart and repairing watches. When he was sixteen Henry walked nine miles into the city of Detroit, and got the first of a series of jobs in machine shops and factories. To him there was beauty and challenge in what to other men was a greasy, if useful, collection of gears, wheels, rods, and valves.

In 1891 Ford got a job as night engineer at the Edison works in Detroit. He was good at his job and within two years was made chief engineer. His life, however, was beginning to center in a little brick shed behind a modest house on Bagley Avenue where he lived with the young wife whom he had married five years before. In that shed, he was working on a gasoline-powered automobile.

Henry Ford was not the only man so occupied. The whole country was feeling its way towards some kind of "horseless carriage." Models driven by electricity or by steam were being put together, but they all faced serious problems of recharging electric batteries, or of carrying heavy steam boilers. The key to the automobile's future lay in the lightweight internal combustion engine, which burned a mixture of air and vaporized fuel, and was its own source of power. Such lightweight and efficient engines had been developed by a number of men between 1860 and 1890—Belgian Etienne Lenoir, Germans Gottfried Daimler and Nikolaus Otto, and American George B. Brayton. During the 1890's, loud poppings and explosions were heard from barns and backyard workshops as pioneers like Edgar and Elmo Apperson, Charles and Frank Duryea, Ransom E. Olds, and Elwood Haynes built benzine, naphtha, kerosene, and gasoline engines and hitched them to homemade buggies.

Like all of them, Ford had to make up his own rules as he went along. In

ALL: HORNUNG, CLARENCE, *Gallery of the American Automobile*, 1965

QUADRICYCLE

"A" TONNEAU

"K" TOURING CAR

Ford's initial car, the 1896 Quadricycle, featured a motor made with odd metal scraps and a plumber's pipe. Many experiments later the first "A" tonneau, capable of 30 m.p.h., rolled out of Detroit in 1903. The "K" touring car appeared in 1906, priced at $2,500; barely one thousand were made. Ford's phenomenal success came with his "universal car," the 1908 Model T.

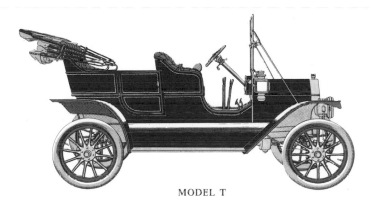

MODEL T

1892 or 1893 he built a motor. The test bed was the kitchen sink, the electric power for the spark-plug came from an overhead socket, and Mrs. Ford dripped the gasoline into the carburetor by hand. Through the long months of trial and error Ford worked on building a four-wheel chassis and hooking an engine onto it. Early one morning in 1896 he knocked out part of the wall of the shed, hauled out the first Ford-made automobile, and proceeded to drive it down the still-dark street. It was a two-cylinder affair, weighing five hundred pounds. Chain-driven and steered by a tiller, the primitive vehicle—called a Quadricycle by Ford— held three gallons of gas in its tank. It was the first of some thirty million cars that would carry Ford's name around the world in the years before World War II.

After making a second and a third model car, Ford was already conceiving the idea of large-scale manufacture. He was not alone. Nearly a hundred companies were being formed to make horseless carriages just before 1900. (Few survived competition for any length of time.) He worked endlessly on plans for turning what looked like a buggy without horses into an automobile. In 1899 and again in 1901 he found backers willing to support him. But they were anxious to produce quickly and make profits. Ford wanted to turn every nickel of earnings from sales back into experiments on an improved car. Profit was never as important to him as finding a way to make the best possible car at a price that would attract hordes of buyers. Ford was less concerned with immediate customers than with future drivers.

Since at the start he had to interest the country in the possibilities of a new means of transportation, he did what others were doing. Though he personally cared little for speed, auto races attracted public attention. He built a car in 1902 named "999," and hired a racing driver, Barney Oldfield, who won a five-mile heat driving nearly sixty miles an hour. (A year later, Ford himself drove a new car, his Model B, to a record mile in 39.2 seconds.)

Finally, early in 1903, ten Detroiters with a dash of sporting blood put up enough money to buy half the stock of the Ford Motor Company, capitalized at $100,000. Ford and Alexander Malcolmson, his racing backer, divided the other half between them. How good a gamble this was is shown by the case of a woman who had bought a single share for $100. She earned $95,000 in dividends over a period of sixteen years, and finally sold her holdings for $260,000. (As the company grew it followed a common custom of splitting the stock— doubling the number of shares held by each investor—so that, in time, her

Careening racing cars, depicted in a 1909 Indianapolis Speedway poster, needed the services of a riding mechanic as well as a driver. Ford said of his 999 racer, "The roar alone . . . was enough to half kill a man."

130

COAST TO COAST

Ford regarded racing as a means of proving his cars to the public, and when a New York-to-Seattle race was announced in 1909, he immediately began preparing two Model T's for the 4,100-mile run. Only four other cars were entered, and when the six racers started on June 1, the two Fords rapidly moved ahead. They made Cleveland in four days, where an overheated radiator momentarily halted No. 2 (above). After St. Louis the rains came, and "for seven days," wrote a driver, "the cars labored through Kansas gumbo and Colorado and Wyoming mud and sand." In one flooded stream a rattlesnake confronted No. 2's mechanic, who hurriedly unlimbered his rifle (above left). On June 23 No. 2 chugged into Seattle, seventeen hours ahead of its nearest rival. There the grimy crew posed for a victory photograph (left), flanked by Ford and Robert Guggenheim, who had put up a $3,500 trophy for the winner.

original certificate became many.) Ford had contributed his services and his patents in return for his original stockholding, and as the company began to make money he was able to buy out several other holders and gain control. Then, Ford went busily ahead with his plans to build a car so cheap and so perfect that it would dominate the market. He had a vision of a car that would not be a luxury, but every man's passport to wherever wheels could go.

Before his company was ten years old Ford had hit upon the formula for greatness. He created a standard-ized product. In 1908 he showed the first Model T automobile. It was simple, basic, and black. Almost any amateur handyman could repair it. Its spare parts were few and easily available from Ford dealers—jokers said that substitutes could be found in any dime store. It had neither speed, nor beauty, nor gadgets. But people came to regard it almost as a member of the family. Tin Lizzie, they called it—and took it out on Sundays to show off to their friends; then piled it full of sample cases of farm produce on weekdays, and drove it mercilessly over roads that would have mired an

In 1910 horse-drawn wagons and carriages outnumbered automobiles at Detroit's busiest intersection. However, cars parked on a city street no longer attracted gaping crowds.

ox. The 1909 model sold for $950. By 1926 that price had fallen to approximately $290, and Ford had made and sold over fifteen million Model T's.

He achieved this by adapting an old technique, the assembly line. Whoever invented it—and claims went back even beyond Eli Whitney and his Connecticut arms factory of the early 1800's—Ford and his talented assistants perfected it. Soon the nation got used to pictures of an automobile frame moving slowly along a line of men who stood before piles of parts. Piece by piece, it took shape as a finished car. The time of assembly dropped to under ten minutes. Fords rolled off the line with the effortless rhythm of raindrops drumming on a roof, and in quantities that resembled a deluge.

The Ford Motor Company, by 1914, could put together two hundred cars in a single day. It had 40 per cent of the nation's auto business and earned over $27,000,000. That year the company distributed $12,000,000 in dividends.

For Ford this was proof that his formula worked. A constant, endless drive to simplify, speed up, and increase production meant lower unit costs. (A high portion of a manufacturer's spending is not in his raw materials but his machinery. The harder it works, the quicker it earns back its original cost.) These lower costs to the manufacturer should be reflected in lowered prices to the public, which put an automobile within reach of an

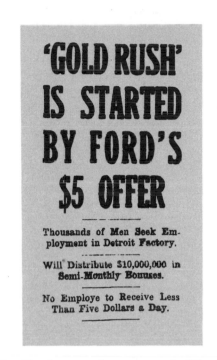

'GOLD RUSH' IS STARTED BY FORD'S $5 OFFER

Thousands of Men Seek Employment in Detroit Factory.

Will Distribute $10,000,000 in Semi-Monthly Bonuses.

No Employe to Receive Less Than Five Dollars a Day.

Headlined across the country, the $5 minimum wage enticed thousands of job seekers. One crowd, turned away by fire hoses, responded by heaving rocks at the factory.

ever increasing number of Americans.

Ford was not only a success, he was also a national symbol. He was thought of as a genius in mechanical production and in efficiency. In Europe and in the United States he was hailed as a man who had succeeded in reducing human effort to a minimum by creating the goods that made life more enjoyable. A world run like a Ford factory would spell plenty for all. Yet not all observers were so cheerful. They pointed out that an assembly-line workman, performing the same operation one hundred times a minute for eight hours a day, was himself reduced to a machine. His work lacked

135

both creativity and craftsmanship. He toiled only in order to buy products, like a car, which would give him back the power and freedom that the factory itself had taken away by turning him into a robot. Though the argument raged on, both those who cheered and those who damned mass production considered Henry Ford the master mechanic who had made a god out of machinery.

Other manufacturers of cars and countless additional products were using his technique, but it was Ford who caught the public eye. This was because of his insistent, outspoken in-

A photograph (left) of the engine assembly line caught Ford, in a business suit, making one of his periodic inspection tours around 1914. Above, magnetos, which supplied electricity to the Model T's spark plugs, take form at Ford's factory in Highland Park.

dividualism. Ford was once quoted (mistakenly, he claimed) as saying "History is bunk." People thought that this showed a lack of respect for learning. It really showed his firm belief that past experience ought never to stand in the way of experiment. His own auto-making experiments were often brilliant. They encouraged him to branch into other fields where he was not always so successful. But he never let the warnings of others hold him back.

When he announced the five-dollar minimum wage on January 5, 1914, most skilled workmen the country over were making only half that amount. His purpose was, he said, to pay workmen enough to buy the products of the assembly line. The next day ten thousand men besieged the factory gates asking for work. For over a week thousands of unemployed swarmed into Detroit, and police had to be called out to prevent mob violence. The Ford company received an additional fourteen thousand applications by mail. Economists predicted doom. Before long, however, the world saw wages catch up with Ford's minimum and pass far beyond it.

On the other hand, Ford tried desperately to get his workmen to give up drinking and smoking, which he believed to be unhealthy and wasteful. But despite the most elaborate system of checks, he found he could not force them to live "efficiently" (as he would have put it) in their off-duty hours.

In 1916 two of the seven remaining

stockholders in the Ford Motor Company brought a spectacular lawsuit against Ford. They insisted that he distribute three quarters of the company's accumulated profits—about $39,000,000—in dividends. Ford had intended to plow them back into improvements that would justify his recent slashing of the Model T's price. At the trial, Ford offered the unusual view that a company's duty was not to make "such awful profits," but "to do as much good as we can, everywhere, for everybody concerned." The case dragged on until, in 1919, the courts decided that an investor who puts up his money does not have to support such generous ideas, and

Life, DECEMBER 30, 1915

·*Ford's earnest but misguided efforts to end World War I drew oceans of laughter from the American press. This caricature of his "Peace Ship" puts three crones in the tub that took the Wise Men of Gotham to sea.*

Ford was made to pay out $20,000,000 in dividends.

For a while Henry Ford bided his time. Then, by threatening to quit the firm and begin building a competing car, he forced his minority stockholders to sell out to him. From 1920 until the mid-1950's, all the stock in the Ford Motor Company was family-owned. Ford was responsible to no one, not even to the banks. When he needed cash quickly, he would force his dealers to take large consignments of autos, which they had not ordered. They had to pay at once or risk losing their dealerships. It was they who had to borrow from the banks.

Ford's urges to improve the manufacture and sale of cars usually were founded in good sense. His ideas about improving the world were less sensible. Late in 1915 he announced that the war raging in Europe was wasteful and immoral, chartered a ship, the *Oscar II*, and sailed for Scandinavia with a shipload of other pacifists. Ford declared he would try to end the conflict and have the soldiers "out of the trenches by Christmas." But he neither said nor in his heart knew how this was to be done. After spending a few days in Europe, he quietly came home again. There was loud laughter, but it died down two years later when the Ford factories made sixty submarine chasers for the United States Navy at a cost of $46,000,000 after America entered the war.

In 1919 Ford sued the Chicago *Tribune* for libel, because the paper had

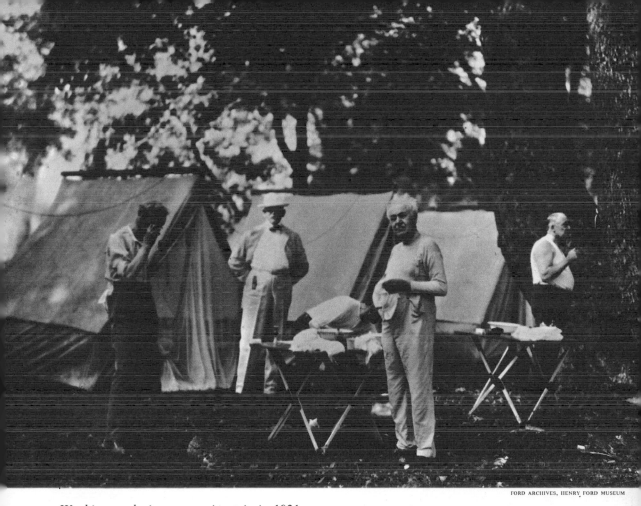

Washing up during a camping trip in 1921 are (from left): Ford, Methodist Bishop W. F. Anderson, tire tycoon Harvey Firestone (leaning over the table), Thomas Edison, and President Warren Harding.

called him an "anarchist" and an "ignorant idealist." On the witness stand, he revealed that he did not know (or would not admit that he knew) who Benedict Arnold was, or when the American Revolution had taken place. He was a genius when it came to production planning, and he simply did not care if anyone thought him an ignoramus about matters that did not interest him. The jury found in his favor, but awarded only a token six

cents in damages. It was their way of saying that calling Ford "ignorant" could not greatly harm his reputation.

Throughout the twenties, Ford conducted crusades through his own newspaper, the Dearborn *Independent.* Some of his campaigns were innocent enough, and condemned only minor sins such as smoking. Others were more serious—like a six-year campaign of slander against the Jewish

OVERLEAF: *Ford extolled the country life, but by 1928—the year of this traffic jam in Maryland—Americans had learned that getting there was not always half the fun.*

139

THE NEW FORD CONVERTIBLE CABRIOLET

Advertisements for the 1931 Model A convertible hinted at wealth and social standing, in sharp contrast to the workhorse Model T, which "could go anywhere but in society." Painted in "a choice of colors to match the season," the Model A was as "smart as tomorrow."

people that finally ended with another lawsuit, then a public apology by Ford, and the killing off of the *Independent*. Nobody knew or ever found out what made him do these things. Unfortunately when Henry Ford had a foolish idea he could afford to put millions into promoting it.

Through the First World War and the twenties Ford's power was growing. To keep the price of automobiles low the company, like others before it, tried to control the prices of its raw materials by buying them and transporting them, too. Ford owned rubber plantations in Brazil and forests in Canada. He owned blast furnaces and mills for rolling his own steel, and plants for making his own glass. He owned ore-carrying steamers, and at

one time he even owned his own railroad, the Detroit, Toledo & Ironton, which brought coal from his mines to his factory. The huge plant at River Rouge, covering 1,200 acres, was one of more than forty Ford assembly plants and parts factories spread over this country, Canada, and Europe. The company began manufacturing tractors that churned up the soil in Iowa and on the steppes of Russia. Ford made airplanes, too, and the tri-motored "Tin Goose" became almost as familiar a sight on the airfields as "Tin Lizzie" was on the roads.

Cars made by Ford and his rivals were affecting American life. To farmers, town was no longer a remote place to be visited twice a year. It was just a few minutes away from home, offering the once-forbidden attraction of the movies, and department stores that made shopping easy. Once teen aged boys or girls could drive a car, they were able to leave chaperones and parents and go off on their own to places of amusement. The old standards were shifting at the speed with which cars rolled out of Detroit factories, or zipped along the highways. Workers no longer had to live clustered around the factories where they worked. Even a common laborer could put up the $300 for a Model T and move to a suburb. Prices of real estate around the great cities soared. Today's problems began to take shape—the crowded highways, and the big cities where people spent their days working but from which they fled at night, leaving city dwelling mainly to the poor and underprivileged who took no active part in helping to run the city's affairs. America was undergoing another revolution, and the thin, energetic Michigan farm boy was, in his way, the greatest radical of his time.

Then a strange, ironic thing happened. Henry Ford, the maker of change, began to resist it and to yearn for what was old. In 1923, as he reached his sixties, the automobile market was growing rapidly. Having a car was taken for granted. The public began asking for frills—color and fancy upholstery—and extra, if costly, conveniences like self-starters. Ford's competitors, selling cars with these features, began to eat into the Model T market. But Ford stubbornly re-fused to change. People *should* want only the simplest, easiest-to-repair, and cheapest car, he reasoned; therefore, they would get only that.

Ford's son, Edsel, then president of the company, pleaded with the old man to allow the Model T to be updated. Not until sales figures showed a marked decline in Ford's mastery of the market did Henry yield. In 1926 the last Model T was made and the next year the Model A made its first appearance. It sold well, and so did most of its successors. But from 1928 on, the Ford Motor Company joined Chrysler and General Motors as only one of the "Big Three" of auto-making, and not always the biggest.

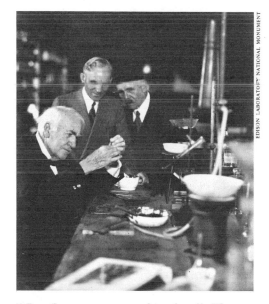

EDISON LABORATORY NATIONAL MONUMENT

"Our floor was never this clean" Thomas Edison commented on the otherwise precise restoration of his laboratory at Greenfield Village. At the dedication in 1929, Edison (left) posed with Ford and an assistant.

Outside the plant, too, a strange thing happened. Ford's hobby became the collection of antiques. Fine paintings or castles in Scotland were not for him. Nor did he donate generously to good works. (After his death, however, the Ford Foundation was set up, and it today spends hundreds of millions annually to promote education and culture.) Ford chose to lavish time and money on a pet project, the creation of Greenfield Village near Dearborn. Here he set up a kind of museum that patched together actual pieces of the past with modern reconstructions. The courthouse where Lin-

B-24 Liberator bombers stand ready to roll off the assembly line at Ford's Willow Run plant during World War II. During the war years Ford made no civilian automobiles.

coln practiced law in Illinois, a replica of the Virginia cabin in which Booker T. Washington was born, and a genuine Elizabethan shepherd's cottage from England stand life-size on the site. A visitor can wander through the actual Menlo Park laboratory where Edison worked on developing uses for electricity, ride on a Suwanee River steamboat, or watch a Cape Cod windmill turn. In the Henry Ford Museum of Transportation (housed in an exact replica of Philadelphia's Independence Hall) buggies, old airplanes, stagecoaches, diesel locomotives, and streetcars are on display—a legacy from the man who was supposed to have said "History is bunk."

Henry Ford, curiously enough, was determined to preserve something of the America that his wheels had banished forever. As he grew older, he became more strongly opposed to novelty, whether in model design or in worker organization. He fought for years against unionization of his employees and only agreed to this in 1941, long after the other big manufacturers had given in. Ford still detested war and took little interest in the huge Willow Run aircraft production plant the company built to turn out bombers for World War II. He outlived his son Edsel, who died in 1943, and in 1945 he handed over effective management of the company to his grandson, Henry II. The old man's mind seemed to be more and more in the past.

One April night in 1947, huge

In 1943 Ford, eighty years old, and his wife, Clara, sat for this photograph in their fifty-six-room mansion, Fair Lane. Two years later Henry Ford II became the company's president.

floods knocked out power stations in the Dearborn area. Henry Ford lay dying at Fair Lane, the home he had built in the township where he was born. His life flickered out in a room lit by kerosene lamps, which had passed out of use fifty years earlier. It was an ironic end for the man who was the chief agent in destroying forever nineteenth-century patterns of life in the United States.

In the century and a half from the birth of Cornelius Vanderbilt to the death of Henry Ford, machines changed the face of America. A few men realized their potential and used the power of capital to set machines usefully to work. Vanderbilt's was the first great fortune to be made from industry, as distinct from trade, Ford's was the last. The present-day level of income taxes has made it well-nigh impossible that any one man will ever again have a billion dollars at his absolute command. The Ford Motor Company has become a corporation in which the public owns thousands of shares of stock; it is no longer operated at the whim of a czar, but on the carefully prepared advice of experts who report to its directors.

Steam, which knit the country together and gave it the power to produce goods, was Vanderbilt's road to success. Ford's was the strength and utility of the gasoline engine, which powered the automobile and the airplane and altered the shape of society forever. Both the first and the last kings of American transportation were rough and tough, and knew their work from the bottom up. They were lucky that each stood at a historical crossroads when new kinds of energy were being released from coal and petroleum, and that each had the vision to put them to use. Their society was big enough to allow them full rein for their activities, whether useful or destructive.

Now we live in an age when new power—that of the atom—has been released and must be harnessed. Our society has changed; individuals respond to different customs and pressures. No one can say if America will have more captains of industry, or whom they might be. But these earlier men of wealth were a colorful, vigorous group, sometimes deplorable, almost never dull. This country is richer for the massive charitable donations they made and also for the lives they led. Their personalities influenced—for good or ill—the entire course of American history.

Today the sprawling River Rouge plant near Detroit stands as a monument to Ford's vision, successfully uniting varied production elements in a huge industrial complex.

Standard's horse-drawn wagons took oil to retailers in 1911.
STANDARD OIL COMPANY OF OHIO

AMERICAN HERITAGE PUBLISHING CO., INC.

James Parton, *President*

Joseph J. Thorndike, *Editor in Chief*

Richard M. Ketchum, *Editorial Director, Book Division*

Stephen W. Sears, *Editor, Education Department*

Irwin Glusker, *Art Director*

AMERICAN HERITAGE JUNIOR LIBRARY

JOSEPH L. GARDNER, *Managing Editor*

Janet Czarnetzki, *Art Director*

Jean Atcheson, *Assistant Editor*

Mary Leverty, *Picture Researcher*

Annette Welles, *Copy Editor*

Nancy Simon, *Editorial Researcher*

Betsy Sanders, *Editorial Assistant*

ACKNOWLEDGMENTS

The Editors wish to thank the following individuals and organizations for their assistance in the preparation of this book and for making available pictorial material in their collections:

American Petroleum Institute, New York—Helen Kaiser

American Tobacco Company, New York—Paul H. Laric

Automobile Quarterly, New York

Carnegie Corporation of New York—Florence Anderson

Carnegie Institute of Technology, Pittsburgh—Sibley Dittmer

Chicago Historical Society—Mrs. Mary Frances Rhymer

Cleveland Public Library—Janet Sanborn

Great Northern Railway, St. Paul, Minnesota—Frank Perrin

Henry Ford Museum and Greenfield Village, Dearborn, Michigan—Donald Shelley, David Glick, Winthrop Sears

Library of Congress—Virginia Daiker

Museum of Fine Arts, Boston—Elizabeth Riegel

Museum of the City of New York—Mrs. Henriette Beal

New-York Historical Society—Betty J. Ezequelle

New York Public Library—Elizabeth Roth, Wilson Duprey

Rockefeller Foundation, New York—Elizabeth Muhlfeld

State Historical Society of Colorado, Denver—Mrs. Kathleen Pierson

State Historical Society of Wisconsin, Madison—Paul Vanderbilt, William Paul

Jonathan Weisberger, Rochester, New York

FURTHER READING

Adams, Charles Francis, Jr., and Adams, Henry, *Chapters of Erie*. Cornell, 1956.

Allen, Frederick Lewis, *The Great Pierpont Morgan*. Harper, 1949.

Burlingame, Roger, *Henry Ford: A Great Life in Brief*. Knopf, 1955.

Carnegie, Andrew, *Autobiography*. Houghton Mifflin, 1920.

———*The Gospel of Wealth and Other Timely Essays*. Edward C. Kirkland ed. Harvard, 1962.

Carroll, J. C., *Armour and His Times*. Appleton-Century, 1938.

Cochran, Thomas, and Miller, William, *The Age of Enterprise*. Harper, 1961.

Hendrick, Burton J., *The Life of Andrew Carnegie*. 2 Vols. Doubleday, Doran, 1932.

Holbrook, Stewart H., *The Age of the Moguls*. Doubleday, 1953.

———*James J. Hill: A Great Life in Brief*. Knopf, 1955.

Hutchinson, William T., *Cyrus Hall McCormick*. 2 Vols. Appleton-Century, 1935.

Jenkins, John W., *James B. Duke, Master Builder*. Doran, 1927.

Josephson, Matthew, *The Robber Barons*. Harcourt, Brace, 1934.

Kirkland, Edward C., *Industry Comes of Age*. Holt, 1961.

Lane, Wheaton J., *Commodore Vanderbilt*. Knopf, 1942.

Lomask, Milton, *Seed Money, The Guggenheim Story*. Farrar, Straus, 1964.

Myers, Gustavus, *History of the Great American Fortunes*. Random House, 1936.

Nevins, Allan, *John D. Rockefeller, The Heroic Age of American Enterprise*. Scribner's, 1940.

———*Study in Power: John D. Rockefeller, Industrialist and Philanthropist*. 2 Vols. Scribner's, 1953. (Abridged by William Greenleaf as *John D. Rockefeller*, Scribner's, 1959.)

Nevins, Allan, and Hill, Frank E., *Ford: The Times, The Man, The Company*. Scribner's, 1954.

———*Ford: Expansion and Challenge*. Scribner's, 1957.

———*Ford: Decline and Rebirth*. Scribner's, 1963.

O'Connor, Harvey, *The Guggenheims*. Covici, Friede, 1937.

Pyle, Joseph Gilpin, *The Life of James J. Hill*. 2 Vols. Doubleday, 1917.

Richards, William C., *The Last Billionaire*. Scribner's, 1948.

Men like these Chicago metalworkers built America's future as surely as any pioneers.

INDEX

Bold face indicates pages on which illustrations appear